MOOMINPAPPA'S MEMOIRS

Tove Jansson

Moominpappa's Memoirs

TRANSLATED BY
THOMAS WARBURTON

A SUNBURST BOOK
FARRAR STRAUS GIROUX

ALSO BY TOVE JANSSON
Finn Family Moomintroll
Comet in Moominland
Moominsummer Madness
Moominland Midwinter
Moominpappa at Sea

English translation copyright © 1994 by Farrar, Straus and Giroux
Text and illustrations copyright © 1968 by Tove Jansson
All rights reserved
Published in Canada by HarperCollinsCanadaLtd
Printed in the United States of America

Published in Finland as Muminpappans memoarer by Schildts
Forlag, Helsingfors
First American edition, 1994
Sunburst edition, 1994

Library of Congress Cataloging-in-Publication Data
Jansson, Tove. Muminpappans memoarer. English
Moominpappa's memoirs / Tove Jansson ; translated by Thomas
Warburton.—1st American ed.
p.   cm.
Rev. ed. of The exploits of Moominpappa. 1966.
[1. Fantasy.] I. Warburton, Thomas, 1918– . II. Jansson,
Tove. Exploits of Moominpappa. III. Title.
PZ7.J247Moe   1993   [Fic]—dc20   93-50954   CIP   AC

This translation has been made possible by a generous grant from the
Finnish Literature Information Centre.

CONTENTS

PROLOGUE

nce, when Moomintroll was quite small, his father got a cold at the very hottest time of summer. Moominpappa refused to drink warm milk with onion juice and sugar, and he refused to go to bed. He sat in the garden hammock blowing his nose and saying his cigars had a horrible taste, and the lawn was strewn all over with his handkerchiefs. Moominmamma carried them away in a little basket.

When his cold became still worse, Moominpappa moved up to the verandah and seated himself in the rocking-chair, with blankets around him up to his nose, and Moominmamma brought him a substantial rum toddy. Only by then it was too late. The rum toddy tasted just as bad as onion milk, and Moominpappa abandoned all hope and took to his bed in the northern attic room. He had never been ill before and took a very serious view of the matter.

When his throat was at its sorest, he asked Moominmamma to fetch Moomintroll and Snufkin and Sniff, and they all assembled around his bed. He then exhorted them never to forget that they had had the privilege of spending their early lives in the company of a genuine adventurer, and asked Sniff to bring him the meerschaum tram from the chest of drawers in the drawing-room. But Moominpappa was so hoarse that no one understood what he wanted.

When they had tucked him in and pitied him and comforted him and given him some toffees and aspirin and amusing books, they took themselves off and went back out in the sunshine.

Moominpappa remained in bed, greatly vexed, and at last he went to sleep. When he awoke towards evening, his throat was feeling a little better, but he was still vexed anyhow. He rang the dinner bell at his bedside, and Moominmamma climbed upstairs at once to ask him how he was feeling.

"I feel rotten," said Moominpappa. "But no matter. Just at the moment it's important that you take some interest in my meerschaum tram."

"The drawing-room decoration?" said Moominmamma, surprised. "What about it?"

Moominpappa sat up. "Really, don't you know

that it played an important part in my youth?" he
asked.

"Well, it was some kind of lottery prize, wasn't
it?" said Moominmamma.

Moominpappa shook his head, blew his nose, and
sighed.

"Just as I thought," he said. "Now, suppose I had
died from my cold this morning. Then none of you
would have had the least idea of the history of this
tram. Probably the same goes for a lot of other
important matters. I may have told you something
about my youth, but obviously you've forgotten it
all."

"Perhaps some of the lesser details," Moominmamma admitted. "One's memory gets a little
vague with time . . . Would you like your dinner
now? We have vegetable soup and fruit juice."

"Ugh," said Moominpappa gloomily. He turned
his face to the wall with a hollow cough.

Moominmamma sat awhile looking at his back.
Then she said, "I'll tell you what: the last time I
tidied the attic, I found a thick exercise book, quite
unused. Suppose you wrote down the whole story of
your youth?"

Moominpappa did not answer, but he stopped
coughing.

"Wouldn't it be convenient now when you've got
a cold anyway and can't go out?" Moominmamma
continued. "What is it called, memories, when you
write about your life?"

"No, memoirs," said Moominpappa.

"And then you could read to us what you've written," Moominmamma said. "After breakfast, or after dinner, for instance."

"I'll have to take some time about it," exclaimed Moominpappa, pushing the blankets away. "You can't write a book all that easily, believe me. I won't read a word aloud before I have a complete chapter, and I'll read it only to you at first, and afterwards to the others."

"You're probably right," said Moominmamma. She went to look in the attic and found the exercise book.

"How's he feeling?" asked Moomintroll.

"Better," said his mother. "And now you'll have to keep very quiet because your father is starting his Memoirs today."

PREFACE

I Moominpappa am sitting tonight by my window gazing into my garden, where the fireflies are embroidering their mysterious signs on the velvet dark. Perishable flourishes of a short but happy life!

As father of a family and owner of a house, I look with sadness on the stormy youth I am about to describe. I feel a tremble of hesitation in my paw as I hold my memoir-pen poised.

Still, I draw strength from some words of wisdom I have come across in the memoirs of another remarkable personage: "Everyone, of whatever walk in life, who has achieved anything good in this world, or thinks he has, should, if he be truth-loving and nice, write about his life, albeit not starting before the age of forty."

It seems to me that I've achieved quite a lot of good things, and even more things that I believe to be good. Also, I am rather nice, I think, and I like the truth except when it's too boring. I don't quite remember how old I am.

Yes, I'll yield to my family's persuasion and to the temptation of talking about myself, because I admit quite willingly that the prospect of being read all over Moominvalley attracts me very much!

May my simple notes bring delight and instruction to all Moomins, and especially to my son. My memory, once sharp, is perhaps a little dimmed. But with the exception of a few small exaggerations and mistakes that surely only enhance the local colour and the vigour of the story, this autobiography will be quite truthful.

In consideration of the feelings of many persons still alive, I have sometimes exchanged Fillyjonks for Hemulens or Gaffsies for hedgehogs, and so forth, but the talented reader will have no difficulties in understanding what was actually what.

Moreover, in the Joxter the reader will discover Snufkin's mysterious father, and will never hesitate to accept that Sniff is descended from the Muddler.

You, innocent little child, who thinks your father a dignified and serious person, when you read this story of three fathers' adventures you should bear in mind that one pappa is very like another (at least when young).

I feel that I owe it to myself, to my own times, and to my descendants to render an account of our remarkable youth, which was not lacking in adventures. And I believe that many of my readers will thoughtfully lift their noses from the pages of this book to exclaim, "What a Moomin!" or, "This, indeed, is life!" (Goodness me, how solemn I feel!)*

Lastly, I want to express my heartfelt thanks to the people who most of all contributed to forming my life into the work of art it undisputedly has become: to Hodgkins, to the Hattifatteners, and to my wife, the matchless and exceptional Moominmamma.

THE AUTHOR

MOOMINVALLEY IN AUGUST

*If you are now really set on reading my Memoirs, I suggest that you read them from the beginning once more.

MOOMINPAPPA'S
MEMOIRS

CHAPTER I

In which I tell of my misunderstood childhood, of the first Experience in my life and the tremendous night of my escape, and of my historic meeting with Hodgkins.

Early one cold and windy evening many years ago, a simple shopping bag was found on the doorstep of the Moomin Foundling Home. In the bag lay none other than I, rather carelessly wrapped in newspaper.

How much more romantic it would have been had I been placed instead on green moss in a small, pretty basket!

However, the Hemulen who had built the Foundling Home was interested in astrology (somewhat), and wisely enough she observed the dominant stars at the time of my coming into the world. They indicated the birth of a very unusual and talented

3

Moomin, and the Hemulen accordingly worried about the trouble awaiting her (geniuses are often regarded as being disagreeable, but I must confess that this has never disturbed me).

The position of the stars is a remarkable matter! Had I been born a couple of hours earlier, I would have become a keen poker player, and everyone born twenty minutes after me felt compelled to join the Hemulic Voluntary Brass Band (fathers and mothers cannot be careful enough when starting a family, and I recommend making minute calculations).

Anyhow, when I was lifted out of the shopping bag I sneezed three times in a very peculiar way. It might have signified something or other.

The Hemulen tied a tag to my tail and stamped it with the magical number 13, because she already had twelve foundlings. All of them were grave, tidy, and obedient, because unfortunately the Hemulen washed them more often than she kissed them (she owned the sort of solid character that lacks all the finer nuances). Dear reader, imagine a Moomin-house where all the rooms are placed strictly in a row, foursquare and painted in the same beer-brown colour! You don't believe me? Moomin-houses, you say, should have plenty of the most surprising nooks and secret chambers, stairs, balconies, and turrets? Not this one! And worse: in the night none of us was allowed to get out of bed, to eat, chat, or walk about. (We were barely permitted to pee!)

I was never allowed to take any funny little bugs home with me to keep under my bed. I had to eat and wash at fixed times. I had to carry my tail at an angle of forty-five degrees when saying good morning. Oh, who can talk about such matters without shedding a tear!

I used to stand before the tiny mirror in the hall and look deep into my unhappy blue eyes, trying to penetrate the secret of my life. With my nose in my paws, I heaved sighs such as "Alone!" "Cruel World!" "Fate is my Lot!" and other sad words, until I felt a little better.

I was a very lonely Moominchild, as is often the case with original talents. No one understood me or could make me out, least of all I myself. Of course, I was aware of the difference between me and the other Moomin children. It lay mainly in their deplorable incapacity for wondering and marvelling.

For example, I would ask the Hemulen why everything was just as it was and not the other way round.

"Wouldn't that be pretty indeed," said the Hemulen to this. "What's wrong with things as they are?" She never explained anything, and I felt more and more strongly that she was trying to shrug the whole matter off. "What, when?" and "Who, how?" have no meaning to Hemulens.

Or I asked her why I was I and not someone else.

"Bad luck for both of us! Have you washed your face?" was the Hemulen's reply to this important question.

I continued: "But why are you a Hemulen and not a Moomin?"

"My father and mother were Hemulens, praise be," she replied.

"And their fathers and mothers?" I asked.

"Hemulens!" the Hemulen cried. "And also their fathers and mothers, and all theirs, and so forth and so forth, and now go and wash or I'll be getting nervous!"

"How dreary. Do they never end?" I asked. "Sometime there must have been a *first* father and mother, mustn't there?"

"That's so long ago that nobody cares," said the Hemulen. "And anyhow, why should we end?" (A dim but unavoidable notion told me that the line of fathers and mothers that had to do with myself was something rather exceptional. I wouldn't be surprised if my swaddling-clothes had been embroidered with a royal crown. But alas! old newspapers tell nothing!)

One night I dreamt that I was holding my tail at a wrong angle, namely, seventy degrees, when I said good morning to the Hemulen. I described this nice dream to her and asked if it made her angry.

"Dreams are trash," said the Hemulen.

"How does one know?" I objected. "Perhaps the Moomin in my dream is the real one, and the Moomin who stands here is only something you are dreaming?"

"I'm afraid not! You are very real!" said the Hemulen dejectedly. "I haven't time for you now! You give me headaches! What'll become of you in this un-Hemulic world?"

"I'm going to be famous," I declared earnestly. "And among other things, I'll build a house for little Hemulen foundlings. And I'll let them eat treacle sandwiches in bed and keep grass snakes and skunks under it!"

"They'll never care for that," said the Hemulen. I'm afraid she was right.

So passed my early childhood in quiet and constant wonderment. I was permanently astonished, always repeating my questions of "What, when?" and "Who, how?" The Hemulen and her obedient foundlings avoided me as best they could; the word "why" seemed to make them uneasy. So I wandered alone in the bleak, treeless landscape by the sea near the Hemulen's house, musing over spiders' webs and stars, over the Little Creeps with curled tails that scuttled around in the water pools, and over the wind that blew from different quarters and always smelt different. (I have later learned that a talented Moomin always wonders about things that seem self-evident but finds nothing strange in things that an ordinary Moomin thinks are curious.) It was a melancholy time.

But by and by a change came: I started to muse about the shape of my nose. I put my trivial surroundings aside and mused more and more about myself, and I found this to be a bewitching occupation. I stopped asking and longed instead to speak of my thoughts and feelings. Alas, there was no one besides myself who found me interesting.

Then came the spring that was so important for my development. At first I didn't understand that it was directed towards myself. I heard the usual chirping, whirring, and humming from all who awoke from the winter and now were in a hurry for something. I saw the Hemulen's symmetrical vegetable garden get its start, and everything that came up was crumpled from impatience. New winds were singing at night. The smells were different. They were the smells of change. I sniffed at everything and got growing pains in my legs, but I still had no idea that it was all intended for me.

Finally, one windy morning, I had a feeling that
. . . well, I simply had a feeling. And I walked straight
down to the sea that the Hemulen didn't like and
consequently had forbidden us.

An important experience awaited me. For the first
time I saw myself full-length. The bright and shiny
ice was much wider than the Hemulen's hall mirror.
I could see the clouds of the spring sky sailing past
my small, pretty, upright ears. At last I could view
the whole of my nose and the firm, well-rounded rest
of myself all the way down to my paws. The paws
were really my only disappointment: they had a look
of helplessness and childishness that bewildered me.
"However," I thought, "perhaps it will pass with
time. Doubtless my strength is in my head. Whatever I do, I will never bore people. I'll never give
them *time* to look as far down as my paws." Enchanted, I gazed at my reflection. In order to see it
still better, I lay down on the ice on my stomach.

But now I disappeared. Now there was only a
green dimness that dwindled deeper and deeper.
Vague shadows were moving about in the unknown
world that led its secret life under the ice. They
looked threatening and very attractive. A giddiness
came over me and I thought, "To fall down there.
Down among the strange shadows . . ."

The thought was so terrifying that I thought it
once again: "Deeper, deeper down . . . Nevermore!
Only down and down and down."

It made me extremely upset. I rose up and
stamped my feet to see if the ice would hold. It did.

I walked a bit farther out to see if it would hold there, too. It didn't.

Suddenly I hung up to my ears in the cold green sea with my paws helplessly dangling over a bottomless and dangerous darkness. In the meantime the clouds were sailing along in the sky quite calmly, as if nothing had happened.

Perhaps one of the threatening shadows would devour me! It was not impossible that he would take one of my ears along to his children and tell them, "Now, eat up before it goes cold! This is genuine Moomin and not to be had every day!" Or I would float ashore with a tragical clump of seaweed behind one ear, and the Hemulen would weep regretfully and tell everyone she knew, "Oh, he was such a singular Moomin! What a pity I didn't understand it in time . . ."

I was just starting on my funeral when I felt something very cautiously nipping my tail. Everyone who owns a tail knows how careful one is of this special ornament and how instantly one reacts if it is threatened by danger or affront. I laid my enticing dreams aside and was filled with energy. Determinedly I crawled up onto the ice, and then ashore. There I told myself, "Now I have had an Experience. This is the first Experience of my life. I can't possibly stay with the Hemulen any longer. I shall take my fate in my own paws!"

I felt cold all day, but no one asked me why. This fortified me in my resolution. At dusk I tore my bedsheet in long strips and tied them into a rope. I made it fast to the window-sill. The twelve obedient foundlings looked on but didn't say a word, and this hurt me. After evening tea I wrote a farewell letter, taking great care over it. Simply, but with dignity, it said:

> *Dear Hemulen,*
> *I feel that great events await me, and that a Moomin's life is short. So I leave this place. Goodbye. Do not grieve: I shall return one day crowned with laurel wreaths!*
> *Cheerio, and with best wishes,*
> *A Moomin who is unlike others*
> *P.S. I am taking a pot of pumpkin mash along.*

The die was cast! Led by the stars of my fate, I went on my way, with never an inkling of the strange events that lay in wait for me. I was simply a very young Moomin, gloomily wandering over the heath, sighing in desolate gorges, my loneliness increased by the terrifying sounds of the night.

At exactly this point in his Memoirs, Moominpappa became very deeply moved by the tale of his unhappy childhood, and he felt that he needed a break. He screwed the top on his memoir-pen and went over to the window. All was silent in Moominvalley.

A light breeze was whispering in the garden and gently swinging Moomintroll's rope-ladder to and fro. "I'm sure I could still manage an escape," Moominpappa thought. "I'm really not so very old!"

He chuckled to himself. Then he lowered his legs over the window-sill and reached for the rope-ladder.

"Hello, Pappa," said Moomintroll at the next window. "What are you up to?"

"Exercises, my boy," answered Moominpappa. "Keeping fit! One step down, two up, one down, two up. Good for the muscles!"

"Better be careful," said Moomintroll. "How are the Memoirs going?"

"Quite well," answered Moominpappa and hauled his trembling legs to safety over the window-sill. "I've just run away. The Hemulen cries with grief. I think it will all be very moving."

"When are you going to read it to us?"

"Soon. As soon as I've come to the river-boat," said Moominpappa. *"It's great fun to read your own book aloud!"*

"I'm sure it is," said Moomintroll and stifled a yawn. *"Well, good night, Pappa."*

"Good night, Moomintroll," said Moominpappa, already unscrewing the top of his memoir-pen.

"Well. Where was I . . . ? Oh, yes, I had run away, and then in the morning—no, that'll come later. I must enlarge upon the night of escape . . ."

All night I wandered through unknown, bleak landscapes. How I pity myself now, afterwards! I didn't dare stop, I didn't dare look around me. Who knows what you may suddenly see in the darkness! I tried to sing "How Un-Hemulic Is This World," the morning march of the foundlings, but my voice trembled so much that it only frightened me all the more. There was a mist that night. Thick as the Hemulen's oatmeal porridge, it crawled over the heath, changing bushes and stones into formless monsters—they glided towards me, reached out for me . . . Oh, how sorry I felt for myself!

Even the redoubtable company of the Hemulen would have comforted me just then. But as for turning back—never! Not after such an imposing letter of farewell.

Dawn came at last.

And at sunrise something beautiful happened. The mist became as rosy-red as the veil on the Hemulen's Sunday bonnet. In a moment the whole world turned rosy-red and friendly! I stood motionless and saw the night disappear. I put it clear out of the way. I experienced my first morning, my own and private morning! Dear reader, judge of my happiness and triumph when I tore the hateful tag from my tail and threw it far into the heather! After that I danced the Moomin Dance of Dawning Freedom in the cold, glistening spring morn, with my small, beautiful ears pricked and my nose lifted against the sky.

No more washing by others' orders! No more eating just because it was dinner-time! No more saluting *anybody* other than a King, and no more sleeping in foursquare, beer-brown rooms! Down with the Hemulens!

Up rose the sun, its light sparkling on cobwebs and wet leaves, and among the receding mists I saw the Way. The Way that wound over the heath, out towards the world, forward into my coming life, which would be a life of singular fame and not a bit like anybody else's.

First of all I ate the pumpkin mash and tossed the pot away. Now I was rid of all possessions. There was nothing I had to do, and nothing I could do out of old habit, because everything was completely new and unknown to me. I have never felt better.

This singular feeling lasted until night. I was so filled with myself and my freedom that the coming dark didn't bother me in the least. Singing a song of my own composition with the greatest words (I'm afraid I've forgotten them now), I wandered on straight into the night.

I was met by a wind with a strange, nice smell that filled my nostrils with expectation. I did not know then that this was the smell of the forest, of moss and bracken and a thousand large trees. When I became tired, I curled up on the ground and warmed my cold paws against my stomach. Perhaps I wouldn't build a home for Hemulen foundlings after all. As a matter of fact, they are very seldom found. I lay for a while musing about which it was better to become, a famous person or an adventurer. I decided to be a famous adventurer. And just before I went to sleep I thought, "Tomorrow!"

When I awoke I was looking straight up into a new world that was all green. Understandably enough, I was very surprised, as I had never seen a tree before. They were dizzyingly tall and straight, and they supported a green roof. The leaves swayed gently and glistened in the morning light, and a great many birds were dashing back and forth, screeching with delight. I stood on my head for a moment to calm myself. Then I shouted, "Good morning! Who does this beautiful place belong to? Are there any Hemulens here?"

"Don't bother us! We're busy playing!" the birds cried and threw themselves headlong among the leaves.

I walked farther into the wood. The moss felt warm and very soft, but there were deep shadows under the bracken. Swarms of small creatures such as I had never seen before were jumping and flying about, but of course they were too small to understand serious conversation. At last I met an older hedgehog sitting by herself and polishing a large nutshell.

"Good morning, ma'am!" I said. "I am a lonely refugee who was born under rather special stars."

"You don't say," said the hedgehog, none too enthusiastically. "I'm working. This is going to be a milk-bowl."

"Indeed," I said, and became aware that I was hungry. "Who owns this beautiful place?"

"No one! Everyone!" said the hedgehog with a shrug.

"I, too?" I asked.

"By all means," mumbled the hedgehog and continued polishing her milk-bowl.

"So you're quite sure, ma'am, that this place doesn't belong to some Hemulen or other?" I asked, worriedly.

"A *what*?" said the hedgehog.

Imagine, this happy creature had never come across a Hemulen!

"A Hemulen has terribly large feet and no sense of humour," I explained. "She has a protruding, slightly depressed snout, and her hair grows in indefinite tufts. A Hemulen does nothing because it would be fun to do it, but only because it must be done, and she tells one all the time what one ought to have done and—"

"Good gracious!" cried the hedgehog and backed away among the bracken.

"Well," I thought, a little huffily (because I'd have liked to tell her a lot more about Hemulens). "This place belongs to nobody and to everybody, so it's mine, too. Now what shall I do?"

The idea came to me all at once, as is usually the case. I just hear a faint "click," and there it is. Given a Moomin and a Place, there simply must follow a House. What a thrilling thought: a house of mine, built by myself! A house exclusively my own! A little farther off I found a brook and a green little glade that appeared very suitable for a Moomin. There was even a small sandy beach by a bend in the brook.

I took a stick and started to draw my house in the sand. I didn't hesitate for a moment, I knew exactly what a Moominhouse should look like. It was high and slender and adorned with several balconies, stairs, and turrets. Upstairs I made three small rooms and a closet for odds and ends, you know, but downstairs was only a single, large, magnificent drawing-room. Outside it I put a glassed-in veran-dah, where I was going to sit in my rocking-chair and look at the brook flowing along, with an enor-

mous glass of juice and a long row of sandwiches by my side. The verandah balustrade was very nicely decorated with a pine-cone pattern. I adorned the pointed roof with a beautiful onion knob and decided to gild it later on. I wondered how to manage the traditional brass door, a relic from the time when all Moomins lived behind porcelain stoves (before someone went and invented central heating). I finally decided to leave out the brass door, and instead I built a large porcelain stove in the drawing-room.

The house as a whole unmistakably resembled a porcelain stove. I was enchanted by my beautiful house that had come into being with such mysterious speed. That must have been because of my inherited ability but also because of talent, sound judgement, and self-criticism. But as one should never praise one's own achievements, I have given you only a simple description of the result.

Suddenly I noticed that I was cold. The shadows had crept out from under the bracken. Night was coming on.

I felt quite dizzy from weariness and hunger, and I couldn't think of anything but the hedgehog's milk-bowl. And perhaps she would have some gold paint to lend me for the roof knob . . . On stiff, tired legs I walked back through the darkening wood.

"Here you are again," said the hedgehog, who was washing dishes. "Only don't talk about Hemulens!"

I spread my paws and replied, "Hemulens,

ma'am, do not interest me any more. I have built myself a house! A modest two-storied house. And now I'm very tired and very happy and most of all terribly hungry! I'm accustomed to eat at five o'clock. And I should need a little gold paint for the knob on—"

"Gold paint indeed!" the hedgehog interrupted sourly. "My new sour milk isn't ready yet, and I have eaten the old. I'm in the middle of washing up."

"Oh, well," I said, "a little milk is neither here nor there to an adventurer. But pray, ma'am, stop this washing up and come and take a look at my new house!"

The hedgehog gave me a suspicious look, sighed, and dried her paws on a towel. "All right," she said. "I'll have to heat the water again. Where is this house? Is it far?"

I led the way, and while I walked I began to have a nasty feeling crawling up my legs and into my stomach. We came to the brook.

"We-ell?" said the hedgehog.

"Ma'am," I said miserably and pointed at the drawing in the sand, "I've planned it like this . . . with a pine-cone pattern in the verandah fret-work. That is, if you could lend me a fret-saw." I was quite confused.

Dear reader, as you must understand, I had entered so powerfully into the building project that I had really thought that the house was finished! This is undoubtedly the mark of a very strong imagination, a characteristic that was to stamp all my future life, as well as the lives of those around me.

The hedgehog didn't say anything. She gave me a very lingering look, mumbled something that I was probably lucky not to catch, and went off to wash more dishes.

I stepped into the brook, and without thinking of anything at all, I began wading downstream in the cool water. The brook ran as brooks do, with many freaks and no hurry. Sometimes it rippled along, clear and shallow, over lots and lots of pebbles, and sometimes it deepened and became dark and quiet. The sun was very low and quite red. It shone on me between the pines, and I shut my eyes and waded along.

At last there was a "click" once again: I had a new thought. If I actually had built the house on that nice little meadow with all its flowers, then it would have spoiled the meadow, wouldn't it? The house ought to have been built *beside* the glade, and beside it there really was no room for a house, you see. And just think that now I would be a house-owner. Is it possible for a house-owner to be an adventurer? Impossible, I'd say.

And further: I could have had people like the hedgehog for neighbours all my life! Probably she belonged to a large clan of hedgehogs of the same kind. As a matter of fact, I had avoided three disasters and ought to be deeply grateful.

Now, afterwards, I count this house-building as the first real Event of my life and believe it to have been of the greatest importance to my development.

Anyway, with my liberty and self-respect preserved, I waded along until my thoughts were interrupted by an odd little sound. In the middle of the
brook a beautiful water-wheel was spinning, made
from twigs and stiff leaves. I halted in surprise. The
next moment I heard somebody saying, "It's an
experiment. Counting the revolutions." I screwed up
my eyes against the red sun and saw a pair of rather large ears sticking out of the blueberry bushes.

"With whom have I the honour of speaking?" I
asked.

"Hodgkins," said the owner of the ears. "And
who are you?"

"A Moomin," I said. "A refugee, and born under
rather special stars."

"What stars?" asked Hodgkins, clearly interested,
and this made me very happy because it was the first
time anybody had put an intelligent question to me.

So I climbed out of the brook and sat down beside
Hodgkins, and without being interrupted a single
time I told him about all the signs and forebodings
that had accompanied my coming into the world. I
told him about the pretty little basket of leaves I lay
in when the Hemulen found me. I told him about
her terrible house and of my misunderstood childhood. Then I went over my adventure on the spring
ice and my dramatic escape and described the gruesome wanderings over the heath.

Hodgkins listened gravely and wiggled his ears at
the right moments. When I finished he thought for

a long time and finally said, "Strange. Rather strange."

"Yes, isn't it," I said thankfully.

"Hemulens are unpleasant," Hodgkins declared. In a preoccupied manner he pulled a packet of sandwiches from his pocket and gave me half of it. "Ham," he said.

Then we sat side by side for a while and saw the sun set and disappear.

During my long friendship with Hodgkins I have often been surprised by his capacity for calming and persuading people without really saying anything of importance or using words beginning with capital letters. It is a bit unjust, but I'll continue my own way of talking.

Anyway, it was a beautiful end to the day, and I recommend everybody with an unruly heart to watch a well-made water-wheel spinning in a brook.

I have later taught my son, Moomintroll, the art of making these wheels. (It's like this: Cut two forked twigs and stick firmly in sandy bottom of stream, some distance apart. Pick four long, stiff leaves, cross to form a star, pierce with stick. Strengthen construction with twigs, as shown in figure. Carefully place stick in forks, and wheel will turn.)

When the wood was quite dark, Hodgkins and I went back to my green meadow for the night. We slept on the verandah, even if he didn't know this. In

any case, the pine-cone pattern was quite clear in my mind. I also knew how to construct the staircase. I was convinced that the house was perfect and also finished, in a way. There was no need to think about it now.

The only thing of importance was that I had found my first friend and consequently begun my life in earnest.

CHAPTER II

Introducing the Muddler and the Joxter in my Memoirs, presenting Edward the Booble, and giving a spirited account of the Oshun Oxtra *and its matchless launching.*

ext morning, when I awoke, Hodgkins was already casting a net in the brook.

"Hello," I said. "Any fish here?"

"No," Hodgkins replied. "A birthday present."

This was a typical Hodgkins reply. What he meant was, simply, that the net was a present from his nephew, who had knitted it himself and might feel sad if it was never used. Gradually I came to know that this nephew was named the Muddler and that his parents had disappeared in a spring cleaning. He now lived in an old coffee tin, of the blue kind, and was a collector, mainly of buttons. All this is rather a brief explanation, isn't it? But even so,

Hodgkins would never have been able to say it all at one single time.

Now he wiggled one of his ears at me and went off through the wood, and I followed him. We stopped at the Muddler's coffee tin. Hodgkins took out a cedarwood whistle that had a pea in it and whistled twice. At once the lid blew off and the Muddler jumped out and rushed towards us with every sign of delight, piping and cutting capers.

"Morning!" he cried. "Why, what fun! Wasn't it today you were going to show me the grand surprise? Whom are you bringing? Goodness me, what an honour! What a pity my tin isn't tidied—"

"Never mind," said Hodgkins. "A Moomin."

"Hello! Welcome! Certainly!" cried the Muddler. "I'm coming . . . Just a moment, please—there are some things I must take along . . ."

And he disappeared into his tin, where we heard him start a terrific rummaging. After a while he came out again carrying a plywood box under his arm, and we all walked together through the wood.

"Nephew," Hodgkins suddenly said, "can you paint?"

"Can I paint!" exclaimed the Muddler. "Of course. I once painted place cards for all my cousins! A separate card for every one! Would you be needing some extra-special de luxe painting with gloss and lustre? Or a maxim for your wall? Excuse me, but what do you need? Is it something to do with your surprise?"

"It's a secret," said Hodgkins.

At this the Muddler became so excited that he started jumping about, and the string around his box snapped, and out tumbled a pile of his personal belongings, including wire springs, suspender belt clasps, a belt punch, ear-rings, electrical plugs, small tins, dried frogs, cheese-knives, cigarette-ends, a great many buttons, and caps from mineral-water bottles, among other things.

"Easy now," said Hodgkins calmingly and helped him to collect it all.

"I had a really splendid piece of string, but I lost it somewhere! I'm sorry!" said the Muddler.

Hodgkins produced a length of rope from his pocket and tied it around the box. We walked on. I could see from Hodgkins's ears that he was secretly excited. At last he halted beside a hazel thicket, turned, and gave us a grave look.

"Is your surprise in there?" the Muddler whispered respectfully.

Hodgkins nodded. We crawled through the hazel bushes and emerged in a clearing. In the middle of it stood a boat, no, a ship!

It was squat and strong, like Hodgkins himself; it looked just as secure and trustworthy. I knew nothing about ships, but I experienced at once a strong feeling of the concept of a ship, so to speak. My adventurous heart started racing and I scented a new kind of freedom. At the same time I had an inner vision of how Hodgkins had dreamt this boat, planned it, and drawn it. I saw him going to this glade every morning to build it. He must have been at it for a terribly long time. But he had told nobody about his ship, not even the Muddler. I suddenly felt sad. I said faintly, "What's it called?"

"The *Ocean Orchestra*," Hodgkins replied. "That's the title of my long-lost brother's book of poems. You'll have to paint the name in ultramarine blue."

"May I? Can I?" the Muddler whispered. "Is it true? Cross your heart? Swear by your tail? Excuse me, but may I paint all of the ship? Do you like red?"

Hodgkins nodded and said, "Be careful of the water-line."

"I've got a large tin of red paint!" the Muddler cried happily. "And a small one of ultramarine . . . How lucky! What fun! Now I'll go home and make you some breakfast and tidy up my tin . . ." And Hodgkins's nephew rushed off, his whiskers trembling with excitement.

HODGKINS' LOST
BROTHER

I looked at the ship and said, "You're quite a carpenter."

At that Hodgkins started talking. He talked a lot, and all of it was about the construction of his ship. He took a piece of paper and a pencil and showed me how the paddle-wheels were to turn. I didn't understand it all, but I saw that he was troubled by something or other. It must have been because of the propeller.

But in spite of the sympathy I

felt, I wasn't able to enter deeply into his problems
—alas, there are a few fields to which my talents do
not extend, and one of them is engineering.

But in the middle of the ship stood a small house
with a pointed roof that aroused a lively interest in
me.

"Do you live in that?" I asked. "It looks like a
Moomin summer-house."

"The pilot-house," Hodgkins said, slightly disapproving.

I fell into thought. The house was too matter-of-
fact to my taste. The window-frames could have
been more imaginative. The captain's bridge would
have been the better for a light balustrade, fret-
worked with marine motifs. And the roof orna-
mented by a knob, perhaps a gilt one . . .

I opened the door. On the floor inside, someone
lay sleeping with his hat over his face.

"Someone you know?" I asked in surprise.

Hodgkins took a look. "The Joxter," he said.

I looked at the Joxter. He was careless in appear-
ance, limp, and more or less smudgily beige in colour. His hat was very old and adorned with wilted
flowers. One had a feeling that the Joxter hadn't
washed for a very long time and didn't intend to.

Just then the Muddler ran up and shouted,
"Breakfast is ready!"

The Joxter awoke and stretched like a cat. "Hup,
pff," he said with a yawn.

"Excuse me, but what are you doing in
Hodgkins's ship?" asked the Muddler menac-

ingly. "Didn't you see the NO ADMITTANCE sign?"

"Certainly," answered the Joxter amiably. "That's why."

This incident showed the Joxter's bent very clearly. The only thing that could awake him out of his sleepy cat-like existence was a notice forbidding him to do something or other, a locked door, or a fence—and if he caught sight of a park keeper his whiskers began trembling and you could expect anything to happen. In between, he mainly slept, or ate, or dreamt. At the time I am writing about, the Joxter was most of all disposed to eat. So we walked back to the Muddler's coffee tin, where a now-cold omelet was resting on a battered chequer-board.

"I had quite a nice pudding this morning," the Muddler explained. "But I can't think where I've put it. This is a sort of instant omelet!"

We were served pieces of it on tin lids, and the Muddler stared expectantly at us as we started eating. Hodgkins chewed in an odd way for a long time and with some effort. Finally he said, "Nephew, something hard."

"Hard!" cried the Muddler. "That must be something from my collection . . . Spit it out! Spit it out!"

Hodgkins deposited a couple of black and bevelled things on his tin lid.

"Oh, *please* excuse me!" cried his nephew. "It's just my cog-wheels. What luck that you didn't swallow them!"

But Hodgkins didn't answer him. He sat frowning and staring before him. The Muddler started to cry.

"Hodgkins, you'll have to forgive your nephew," said the Joxter. "Can't you see that he's really sorry?"

"Forgive him?" cried Hodgkins. "There's no need for that." He took out paper and pencil and showed us where the cog-wheels would fit in to make the propeller and paddle-wheels turn. He drew it like this. (I hope you can see his idea. I'm not quite sure about it.)

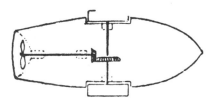

But the Muddler cried, "Oh, is that really true! You need my cog-wheels for your invention!"

We finished our meal in high spirits.

Hodgkins's nephew was so inspired by this event that without losing a minute he donned his largest pinafore and started to paint the *Ocean Orchestra* red. He painted with all his might, and the river-boat became red, and so was the ground around it, and most of the hazel bushes, and never in my life have I seen a redder person than the Muddler himself. But the name of the ship was painted in ultramarine.

When everything was finished, Hodgkins came for an inspection.

"Isn't it beautiful?" the Muddler said nervously. "I've worked very seriously! I've thrown myself into it!"

"I can see that," Hodgkins conceded, looking at his red nephew. He then looked at the water-line and said, "Mphm." Then he looked at the name on the prow and said, "Mphm, mphm!"

"Is the spelling wrong?" asked the Muddler. "Please say something quickly or else I shall start crying again. Excuse me! It wasn't an easy name!"

"The O-s-h-u-n O-x-t-r-a," spelled Hodgkins. He thought for a little while and said, "Take it easy. It'll do."

The Muddler drew a sigh of relief and rushed off to paint his home with the paint that was left.

In the evening, Hodgkins tried his net in the brook. Judge of our astonishment when we found a small binnacle in the net! And inside it an aneroid barometer! I have never stopped wondering about this strange find.

Moominpappa closed his exercise book and gave his hearers an expectant look. "Well, what do you think?" he asked.

"I think it's going to be a terribly fine book," Moomintroll said seriously. *He was lying on his back in the lilac arbour looking at the bumblebees. The weather was warm and calm.*

"But some of that you've just made up," said Sniff.

"Of course not!" cried Moominpappa. "In those days, things really happened! Every word is true!

Naturally, I may have stressed *something or other a little . . ."*

"I wonder," said Sniff. "I just wonder what became of my father's collection."

"What collection?" said Moominpappa.

"Father's button collection," said Sniff. "The Muddler was my father, wasn't he?"

"Certainly," replied Moominpappa.

"Well, then, I'm just wondering about his precious collection. I ought to have inherited it," Sniff pointed out.

"Hup, pff, as my father used to say," said Snufkin. "Why don't you write more about the Joxter? Where is he now?"

"One doesn't always know with fathers," Moominpappa explained with a vague wave of his paw. "They come, they go . . . Anyway, I have saved them for posterity by writing about them."

Sniff gave a snort.

"The Joxter didn't like park keepers either," Snufkin said thoughtfully. "Just think of that . . ."

They all stretched out their legs in the grass and closed their eyes against the sunshine. The weather was nice and sleepy.

"Pappa," said Moomintroll, "did one really talk in that unnatural way in those days? 'Judge of our astonishment,' and 'every sign of delight,' and 'an inner vision,' and so forth?"

"It's not unnatural at all," said Moominpappa gruffly. "Do you think writing is the same as casual conversation?"

"Well, that's the way you do it sometimes," his

son objected. "And you let the Muddler talk ordinarily."

"Never mind!" said Moominpappa. "That's local colour. And, well, there's a lot of difference between what you tell about a thing and what you really think about it. I mean—an opinion or a description's not at all the same if you talk about it, and it all has to do with what you feel and . . . I think . . ." Moominpappa fell silent and turned over some pages of his Memoirs. "Do you think the words I use are too unusual?" he asked.

"It doesn't matter, I believe," said Moomintroll. "That was all so long ago, and one can nearly always guess what you mean. Have you written any more?"

"Not yet," replied Moominpappa. "But there's a thrilling part on its way. I'll come to Edward the Booble and to the Groke. Where's my memoir-pen?"

"Here," said Snufkin. "And let's have more about the Joxter, I say. Don't leave anything out!"

Moominpappa nodded, laid his exercise book in the grass, and took up his pen.

At that time I got my first taste for carpentering. This special talent must have been inborn; I had it in my paws, so to speak. The first achievement was modest, however. I chose an attractive piece of wood at the shipyard (the glade), found a knife, and started to carve the proud ornamental knob that would later adorn the roof of the pilot-house. It was onion-shaped and covered in neat scales, like a fish.

I'm afraid Hodgkins didn't have much to say

about this important detail of the ship's equipment; he had thoughts only for the launching.

The *Oshun Oxtra* was ready. Wonderful to behold and gleaming red in the sunshine, she rested on her four rubber wheels (for clearing treacherous sandbanks). Hodgkins had got himself a gold-braided captain's cap and had crawled under the ship. He was worrying. I heard him mumbling, "She's stuck. Just as I believed. Brilliant, indeed." Hodgkins was talking unusually much while crawling around the *Oshun Oxtra,* a sign of serious concern.

"So you're moving again," said the Joxter and yawned. "Hup, pff! What a life! No end of changing and building up and pulling down again and jumping about. Such a lot of activity may turn out to be really harmful. I'm dejected just to *think* of all the people who work and buzz and bumble about, and of what it all leads to. I had a cousin once who studied trigonometry until his whiskers drooped, and when he had learnt it all, a Groke came and ate him up. Then there he lay in the Groke's stomach, wiser at last!"

The Joxter's pronouncement naturally leads one's thoughts to Snufkin, who later followed the same idle star. Snufkin's mysterious father never worried over things that were really worth worrying about, and he didn't even care about going down to posterity (and indeed he wouldn't have if I hadn't put him into my Memoirs). Anyhow, the Joxter yawned once more and said, "When do we start? Hup, pff."

"Are you coming, too?" I asked.

"Of course," said the Joxter in an astonished voice.

"Please excuse me," said the Muddler, "but as it happens I also had something like that in mind . . . I can't bear to live in my coffee tin any longer!"

"No?" I said.

"That red paint won't dry on sheet-metal!" the Muddler explained. "Excuse me! It gets in my food and in the bed and in my . . . I'm going plumb crazy, Hodgkins, plumb crazy!"

"Better not. Do go and pack," Hodgkins told him.

"Goodness!" cried his nephew. "Dear me, I've lots and lots to do! Such a long journey . . . such a new life . . ." And the Muddler rushed off, leaving a little trail of red paint.

In my opinion, our crew wasn't too reliable.

But the *Oshun Oxtra* was stuck as before: the rubber wheels were deep in the ground, and she didn't move a single inch. We dug up all of the shipyard, but it was to no avail. Hodgkins sat down with his head in his paws.

"Don't grieve, Hodgkins, don't grieve so much," I said.

"I'm not grieving, I'm thinking," Hodgkins replied. "A ship is stuck. You can't push it in the river. Then the river must be brought to the ship. How? You change its course. How? You dam it up. How? You pile stones in it."

"How?" I continued helpfully.

"No!" Hodgkins exclaimed with a force that made me jump. "Edward the Booble. We'll have him sit down in the river."

"Is his behind *so* big?" I asked.

"Bigger," Hodgkins said curtly. "Have you a calendar?"

"No," I said, beginning to feel excited.

"Pea soup, day before yesterday. Bathing day today," mused Hodgkins. "Good. Hurry up, Moomin!"

"Are Boobles savage?" I asked carefully as we walked down along the river beach.

"Yes," Hodgkins replied. "But they tread on you only by mistake. Weep for a week afterwards. Pay for the funeral, too."

"No great help if you're flat," I mumbled, feeling rather brave. (I ask you, dear reader, isn't it easy enough to be brave if you're not afraid?)

Hodgkins suddenly stopped and said, "Here."

"Where?" I wondered. "Does he live in this tower?"

"That's his leg," Hodgkins explained. "Keep quiet now—I'll have to shout." Then he shouted at the top of his voice, "Ahoy, up there! Hodgkins down here! Mr. Edward, where are you bathing today?"

And a thunder somewhere in the sky answered, "In the sea, as always, you sand-flea!"

"Try the river! Sand bottom! Nice and soft!" roared Hodgkins.

"Lies and trumpery," said Edward the Booble.

"Every mouseling knows that this grokely river is choked with grokely stones!"

"No! Sand bottom!" Hodgkins yelled.

The Booble grumbled to himself for a bit, and then he said, "All right, I'll bathe in your grokely river. Get out of my way—I haven't the money for any more funerals. And if you've tricked me, you wood-louse, you'll have to pay for it yourself! You know I have such sensitive feet. Not to speak of my behind!"

Hodgkins whispered one single word: "Run!"

And we ran. I've never run faster in my life, and all the time I imagined Edward the Booble lowering his enormous behind down among the sharp stones, and his titanic wrath, and the gigantic flood he would doubtless stir up, and all this looked so big and dangerous that I gave up every hope.

Suddenly—a roar to make your neck bristles rise! And then a terrific whoosh! The flood wave came weltering through the wood . . .

"All aboard!" cried Hodgkins.

We ran into the shipyard with the flood wave at our heels, only barely got our tails inside the rail, stumbled over the Joxter, who was asleep on the deck—and then everything was drowned in a cascade of white foam. The *Oshun Oxtra* stood on her ears, so to speak, and she creaked and groaned from dread.

But the next moment the proud ship straightened up over the moss; she lifted and made good headway through the wood. The paddles swished, the screw turned—our cog-wheels were functioning perfectly! With a steady paw Hodgkins took the helm and steered us safely between the trees.

What a matchless launching! Blossoms and leaves were raining upon the deck, splendidly adorning the *Oshun Oxtra* for her final triumphant leap into the river. With happily splashing paddles, she swept out into the middle of the stream.

"Look out for sandbanks!" shouted Hodgkins (he wanted to run over one to try out his hinge-and-wheel construction). I gazed intently over the river but saw only a red tin bobbing about at some distance ahead.

"Some sort of tin," I said.

"That reminds me of something," said the Joxter. "There might be some sort of Muddler in it."

I turned to Hodgkins. "You forgot your nephew!"

"Indeed. How could I have?" Hodgkins said.

Soon we saw the Muddler's red, wet face appearing over the rim of the tin. He flapped his arms and ears wildly and was obviously in danger of strangling himself in his scarf.

The Joxter and I leant over the rail and took hold of the tin. It was still quite sticky with paint and rather heavy.

"Mind the deck," said Hodgkins when we hoisted the tin aboard. "How do you feel, dear nephew?"

"I'm going crazy!" cried the Muddler. "Think of it! Flood waves in my packing . . . Everything downside-up! I've lost my best window-catch and probably the pipe-cleaner, too. My nerves are all unsorted, and so is my collection . . . Oh, what a fate!"

And the Muddler began rather happily to arrange his button collection by a new system, while the *Oshun Oxtra* continued peacefully gliding, gently splashing along down the river. I sat beside Hodgkins and said to him, "I really hope we'll see no more of Edward the Booble. Do you think he's very angry with us by now?"

"Very," replied Hodgkins.

CHAPTER III

Recapitulating my first heroic rescue feat, its stagger-
ing outcome, a few thoughts, and a description of the
behaviour of Niblings.

own the river we went, leaving the green
and friendly woods behind us. Everything became large and tremendous,
and strange, ugly animals wandered bellowing and sneezing along the steep
river banks. It really was a lucky thing for the *Oshun
Oxtra* to have a couple of responsible persons
aboard, namely, Hodgkins and myself. The Joxter
took nothing seriously, and the Muddler's main interest never reached far from his tin. We had put it
on the foredeck, and it was slowly drying in the
sunshine. But we never quite succeeded in cleaning
up the Muddler himself; he remained slightly pink
for as long as I knew him.

The river-boat was slowly splashing along,

adorned with my gilded roof-knob. Naturally, Hodgkins had some gold paint aboard his ship; I'd have been surprised indeed if he hadn't been equipped with this important requisite.

Most of the time I sat in the pilot-house, looking at the passing river banks in all their oddity, tapping the aneroid barometer now and then, or taking a little exercise pacing back and forth on the bridge, lost in my thoughts.

I especially liked to think about the Hemulen. How impressed she would have been to see me an adventurous part-owner of a river-boat. As a matter of fact, it would have served her right!

One evening we made our course into a deep and lonely bay.

"I don't like the look of this bay," remarked the Joxter. "It gives me Forebodings."

"Forebodings!" said Hodgkins with an indescribable intonation. "Nephew! Let go the anchor."

"Aye, aye, sir. At once, sir!" cried the Muddler, and promptly tossed our kettle overboard.

"Did it have our supper in it?" I asked.

"I'm afraid it did!" cried the Muddler. "Excuse me! So easy to grab the wrong thing! I was so excited . . . But I'll give you some jelly instead—if I can find it . . ."

This kind of occurrence is very characteristic of Muddlers.

The Joxter stood at the rail and looked at the shore with gleaming eyes. Dusk was quickly falling over the mountain ridges that stretched, row after desolate row, to the horizon.

"Well, what about your Forebodings?" I asked.

"Hush!" said the Joxter. "I heard something out there . . ."

I cocked my ears but heard only the faint land breeze soughing in the rigging.

"It's nothing," I said. "Come along inside; we'll light the kerosene lamp."

"I found the jelly!" cried the Muddler and jumped out of his tin with a dish in both hands.

At that moment a desolate sound cut through the evening calm, a threatening wail that raised the neck bristles of us all. The Muddler cried out and dropped his dish with a crash.

"That's the Groke," said the Joxter. "She's singing her hunting song tonight."

"Can she swim?" I asked.

"Nobody knows," replied Hodgkins.

The Groke was hunting in the mountains. Her wail was the most lonely sound I have ever heard. It diminished, it came nearer again—it disappeared at times. It was even worse when she was silent. You could easily imagine her shadow racing along over the ground in the light of the rising moon.

It became cold on deck.

"Look!" the Joxter cried.

Somebody came tearing down to the water and began darting to and fro on the bank.

"That one," said Hodgkins glumly, "is going to be eaten alive."

"Not before the eyes of a Moomin!" I cried. "I'm going to save him!"

"You won't have time," said Hodgkins.

But I had made my decision. I stepped up on the rail and said, "An unknown adventurer doesn't ask for wreaths on his grave. But I'd appreciate a granite monument with two weeping Hemulens!" Whereupon I dived into the black water and came up under the Muddler's kettle with a clonk, with great presence of mind scooped out the Irish stew, and then set my course straight as a torpedo to the shore, pushing the kettle along before me with my nose.

"Courage!" I cried. "The Moomins are coming! There's something rotten in a country that allows its Grokes to eat anybody they like!"

Pebbles and stones were rattling up in the mountain . . . The Groke's hunting song had ceased; now only a hot panting was to be heard, nearing, nearing . . .

"In the kettle!" I cried to the unfortunate one.

He made a jump, and the kettle sank to its handles. Somebody reached for my tail in the darkness . . . I pulled it away . . . Ho! Glorious feat! Lonely deed! I started on the heroic journey back towards the *Oshun Oxtra,* where my friends stood waiting, breathless with excitement.

The rescued person was heavy, very heavy.

I swam with all my might, using a rotating tail stroke and rhythmic stomach movements. Like a Moomin wind I swept along, was hauled aboard, tumbled down on the deck, and emptied the saved person from the kettle, while the Groke stood howling out her disappointment and hunger on the shore (because, in fact, she couldn't swim).

Then Hodgkins lit the kerosene lamp to see whom I had rescued.

I believe this was one of the worst moments of my stormy youth. Because on the wet deck before me sat none other than—the Hemulen! As one used to say in those days: "What a tableau!"

I had rescued the Hemulen.

In my initial fright I raised my tail at a forty-five-degree angle, but the next moment I remembered that I was a free Moomin and said nonchalantly, "Really! I say! Quite a surprise! I'd never have believed that!"

"Believed what?" asked the Hemulen, and shook some Irish stew out of her umbrella.

"That I'd rescue you, Auntie," I said agitatedly. "I mean, that your life would be saved by me. I mean, did you get my farewell letter?"

"I've never seen you before, young man," said the Hemulen reservedly. "Nor have I had any letter from you. You probably forgot to put a stamp on it. Or wrote the wrong address. Or forgot to put it in the post box. *If* you know how to write . . ." She adjusted her hat and added graciously, "But you're no mean swimmer."

"Do you two know each other?" the Joxter carefully asked.

"No," said the Hemulen. "I'm the Hemulen's Aunt. Who's been slopping jelly all over the floor? Bring me a rag, you there with the ears. I'll clean it up for you."

Hodgkins (because it was he whom she meant) rushed forward with the Joxter's pyjamas, and the Hemulen Aunt proceeded to scrub the deck with them.

"I'm cross," she explained. "And at such times the only thing that helps is tidying up."

We watched her in silence.

"Didn't I tell you of my Forebodings?" mumbled the Joxter finally.

At this the Hemulen Aunt turned her ugly snout towards us and said, "Quiet, you there, please. You're much too small to smoke. You ought to drink milk—that's healthy—and it would save you from shaky paws, a yellow nose, and a bald tail. Rescuing me was a great stroke of luck for you all. We're going to keep things in order here!"

"Must take a peek at the glass," Hodgkins said quickly. He slunk into the pilot-house and locked the door behind him.

The aneroid barometer had fallen forty notches from pure fright and didn't dare go up again until after the affair of the Niblings. I'll tell you presently about that.

But as yet we had no hope of avoiding a time of tribulation I'm convinced none of us had earned.

"Well, that's how far I've come," said Moominpappa in his natural voice, and looked up from his Memoirs.

"You know," said Moomintroll, "I'm beginning to get accustomed to those strange turns of phrase you're using all of a sudden. That must have been a big kettle you had . . . Are we going to be rich when your book is finished?"

"Terribly rich," Moominpappa answered earnestly.

"Then I think we ought to share the money," Sniff proposed. *"After all, you've taken my father the Muddler for your hero!"*

"But the Joxter's the hero," said Snufkin. *"Just think that I'm only now getting to know what a splendid father I had! It feels good that he resembles me."*

"Your old fathers are simply so much background!" Moomintroll cried, and gave Sniff a kick under the verandah table. *"They should be glad they're put in at all!"*

"You kicked me!" cried Sniff, his whiskers bristling.

"What are you up to?" asked Moominmamma at the drawing-room door. *"Is anybody annoyed over anything?"*

"Pappa's reading about his *life,"* Moomintroll explained, stressing the *"his."*

"Well, how do you like it?" asked Moominmamma.

"Thrilling!" said her son.

"Yes, isn't it," Moominmamma agreed. *"Only don't read anything that could give the youngsters a bad impression of us. Just say 'dash, dash, dash' instead at such places. Do you want your pipe?"*

"Don't let him smoke!" cried Sniff. *"The Hemulen Aunt says smokers get shaky paws, a yellow nose, and a bald tail!"*

"I'm not so sure," said Moominmamma. *"He's smoked all his life, and he's not shaky, yellow, or bald. All nice things are good for you."*

And she lit Moominpappa's pipe for him and

opened the window to the evening breeze. Then she went whistling out to the kitchen to brew some coffee.

"How could you forget the Muddler at the launching!" Sniff said reproachfully. "Did his button collection ever get sorted again?"

"Oh, many times," answered Moominpappa. "He was always inventing new systems. He arranged them by colour, by size, by form, by material, and by how much he liked them."

"Wonderful," said Sniff dreamily.

"What worries me is that my father had his pyjamas full of jelly," Snufkin said. "Then what did he sleep in?"

"In mine," said Moominpappa, and puffed out large clouds of smoke towards the ceiling.

Sniff yawned. "Want to come bat-hunting?" he asked.

"All right," said Snufkin.

" 'Bye, Pappa," said Moomintroll.

Moominpappa remained on the verandah. He sat thinking for a while, then took out his memoir-pen and continued the story of his youth.

Next morning the Hemulen Aunt was devastatingly cheerful. At six o'clock we awoke to her trumpeting: "Good morning! Good morning!! Good morning!!! Now's the time to start! What about a little sock-darning contest (because I've looked in your drawers). Then some educational games as a reward. *Very* useful. And what's the healthful fare today?"

"Coffee," said the Muddler.

"Porridge," said the Hemulen Aunt. "Coffee's for the old and shaky."

"I knew a chap once who died of porridge," mumbled the Joxter. "It stuck in his throat and choked him."

"I wonder what your parents would say if they saw you drinking coffee," said the Hemulen Aunt. "They'd *weep*. But I suppose you're badly brought up. Or not brought up at all. Or born impossible to bring up."

"I was born under special stars," I took the opportunity of saying. "I was found in a small sea shell padded with velvet."

"I don't want to be brought up," Hodgkins said very distinctly. "I'm an inventor. I do what I like."

"Excuse me!" cried the Muddler. "But my parents don't weep, ever! They were lost in a spring cleaning."

The Joxter filled his pipe with menacing gestures. "Hah!" he said. "I don't like *decrees*. They make me think of park keepers."

The Hemulen Aunt gave us a long, long look. Then she slowly said, "From now on, I'm going to take care of you."

"You needn't," we all shouted.

But she shook her head and pronounced the terrible words: "It is my Hemulic Duty," and then she vanished forward, undoubtedly to think up something educational and infernal.

We curled up under the sun tent in the stern and tried to comfort one another.

"By my tail!" I said. "I swear never to save any-body in the dark again."

"Too late now," said the Joxter. "This here Aunt may do anything. One of these days she'll throw my pipe overboard and put me to work! I'm sure there are no limits to what she can do."

"Maybe the Groke'll be back?" whispered the Muddler hopefully. "Or somebody else who'll be so kind as to eat her? Excuse me! Was that rude of me?"

"Yes," said Hodgkins. After a while he added earnestly, "But there is something in it."

We lapsed into silence and self-pity.

"If I only were a great man!" I said. "Great and famous! Then an aunt like that would be no matter!"

"How does one become famous?" asked the Muddler.

"Oh, that must be rather easy," I said. "You have only to do something no one else has hit upon before . . . Or something well known in a new way . . ."

"For instance?" said the Joxter.

"A flying river-boat," mumbled Hodgkins, and his small eyes lit up with astonishing brightness.

"I believe it's a bore to be famous," declared the Joxter.

"Perhaps it's fun at first, but then you get used to it, and soon it makes you sick. Like on a merry-go-round."

"What's that?" I asked.

"An engine," Hodgkins said eagerly. "You have cog-wheels and mount them like this, intersecting." And he took out pen and paper.

Hodgkins's deep devotion to machinery was something that never ceased to astonish me. Engines bewitched him. For my part, I find them more or less unsettling. A water-wheel is funny and understandable, but even a zipper is near enough to the world of machinery to make me slightly distrustful. The Joxter knew somebody who had a zipper in his trousers, and one day the zipper stuck, and nobody could open it again, ever. Terrifying!

I was just about to communicate my thoughts on zippers to the others when we heard a very strange sound.

It was a low, half-muffled howl, like somebody bellowing through a tin tube far away. Its tone was definitely menacing.

Hodgkins looked out from the sun tent and uttered the single, ominous word: *"Niblings!"*

Here a short explanation may be necessary, although all sensible people know most of these facts. While we were having a rest under the sun tent, the *Oshun Oxtra* had slowly drifted down to the river mouth, where the Niblings lived. The Nibling is a social animal and detests being alone. He lives under river beds, burrowing and digging tunnels with his eye-teeth, and forming rather happy colonies. Niblings have suckers on their feet and leave sticky tracks, which is why some people, quite wrongly, call them Sticklings.

The Nibling is mostly good-natured, except that he cannot keep himself from chewing and gnawing at things, particularly at things he has never seen before. Also he has one more unfortunate trait: he will chew off the nose of a person if he thinks it too big. So (for obvious reasons) some of us felt a little nervous.

"Stay in the tin!" Hodgkins cried to his nephew.

The *Oshun Oxtra* lay quite still amid a great swarm of Niblings. They looked us over with their round blue eyes, while menacingly waving their whiskers and treading water.

"Please make way for us," said Hodgkins.

But the Niblings only drew closer around the river-boat, and then a couple of them started to climb the side with their suckered feet. When the first one poked its head over the rail, the Hemulen Aunt appeared from behind the pilot-house.

"What's all this?" she asked. "Who are those fellows? I can't have them coming aboard to disturb our educational games!"

"Don't frighten them! They'll be angry," Hodgkins said.

"*I'm* angry!" cried the Hemulen Aunt. "Away! Away! Be off with you!" And she started hitting the nearest Nibling over its head with her umbrella.

At once all the Niblings turned to look at the Hemulen Aunt, and it was obvious that they were contemplating her nose. When they had contemplated it long enough, they once more emitted their curious muffled tin-tube bellow. And then everything happened very fast.

Niblings came swarming aboard by the thousands. We saw the Hemulen Aunt lose her balance and be carried off, wildly waving her umbrella, on a living carpet of hairy Nibling backs. With a few loud screams she was tipped over the rail, and the whole party disappeared to a destination unknown.

All was silent and peaceful once again, and the *Oshun Oxtra* paddled along as if nothing had happened.

"We-ell," said the Joxter. "Aren't you going to rescue her?"

My chivalry prompted me to rush to her aid, but my bad and natural instincts told me that it wasn't necessary. I mumbled something about its being too late. And so it was, indeed.

"Mphm," said Hodgkins a little uncertainly.

"And so much for her," said the Joxter.

"A sorry story," I said.

"Excuse me, was that my fault?" asked the Muddler sincerely. "I hoped, didn't I, that somebody would be so kind as to eat her? Is it very bad that we don't grieve for her in the least?"

Nobody answered.

I ask you, dear reader, what would *you* have done in this awkward situation?

I had saved the Aunt *once,* hadn't I, and a Groke really is something very much worse than a Nibling. Niblings aren't so bad, in fact . . . Perhaps she would enjoy the change? Perhaps she would even look nicer with a smaller nose? Don't you think so, too?

However, the sun shone peacefully, and we started to scrub the deck (which was quite sticky from the Niblings' feet), and then we drank enormous quantities of good, strong black coffee. The *Oshun Oxtra* wound its way between hundreds and hundreds of small, flat islands.

"There's no end to them," I said. "Where are we going?"

"Anywhere . . . or nowhere in particular," said the Joxter, and filled his pipe. "What does it matter? We're all right, aren't we?"

I couldn't deny that we were all right, but I longed to arrive somewhere! I wanted something new to happen. Anything, but some new event! (Except, of course, anything to do with Hemulens.)

I had the terrible feeling that a lot of great adventures were continually happening, one after another, at some place where I wasn't—enormous, colourful adventures that would never repeat themselves for me. I was in a hurry, in a great hurry! I sat in the prow looking ahead towards the future, while I pondered over the insights I had derived from my experiences. They were seven so far, namely:

1. *Try to have your Moomin babies born at astrologically suitable moments, and give them a romantic entry into the world! (Positive instance: my talent. Negative instance: the shopping bag.)*
2. *People do not like to hear about Hemulens when they have other things to do. (Positive instance: Hodgkins. Negative instance: the hedgehog.)*
3. *You can never tell what may be caught in a net! (Positive instance: Hodgkins's binnacle.)*
4. *Never paint things anew simply because there is some paint left over. (Negative instance: the Muddler's tin.)*
5. *All big animals are not dangerous. (Positive instance: Edward the Booble.)*
6. *Even small animals can be courageous. (Positive instance: I myself.)*
7. *Try to avoid saving people in the dark! (Negative instance: the Hemulen Aunt.)*

While I sat sorting out these remarkable truths of life, the river-boat rounded the last of the small islands, and suddenly my heart took a leap straight into my throat and stuck there, and I cried, "Hodgkins! Ocean ahead!"

At last something had happened. Straight before me lay the glittering, blue, adventurous sea!

"It's too big," the Muddler said, and vanished into his tin. "Excuse me, it hurts my eyes and I don't know what to think!"

But the Joxter shouted, "How blue and soft it is! Let's steer straight ahead and just roll and sleep and never arrive anywhere . . ."

"Like Hattifatteners," Hodgkins said.

"Like what?" I asked.

"Hattifatteners," repeated Hodgkins. "They just travel and travel . . . No peace, no rest."

"There's the difference," the Joxter contentedly said. "I've got lots of peace and rest! And I like to sleep. The Hattifatteners never sleep, because they can't. And they can't talk either—they just try to reach the horizon."

"Have any of them succeeded?" I asked, shuddering.

"Nobody knows," said the Joxter with a shrug.

We anchored by the rocky coast. Even today, I feel a quiet thrill along my back when I whisper to myself the words "We anchored by the rocky coast." For the first time in my life I saw red rocks and transparent jelly-fish, those strange little balloons that breathe and have a flower-shaped heart.

We went ashore to gather sea shells.

Hodgkins firmly maintained that he was going ashore to take a look at the anchorage-ground, but something tells me that he took an interest in sea shells also. Between the rocks we found hidden little sandy beaches, and imagine the Muddler's joy when he discovered that every small stone was completely smooth and round like a ball or an egg. Filled with the incomparable happiness of the collector, the Muddler snatched the saucepan off his head and gathered and gathered and gathered. The sand was

raked into smooth little ripples under the clear, green water, and the rocks were warm in the sun-shine. The wind had gone home to sleep, and there was no horizon to be seen, only a great transparency of light.

The world was very large in those days, and small things were small in a much nicer way than now, and suited me very much better. If you see what I mean.

At this moment I have discovered a new thought that seems important. An attraction for the sea must be a Moominous quality. I see with satisfaction that my son has inherited it.

But, dear reader, please note that it is, rather, *the beach* that awakens our rapture.

Far out on the sea a normal Moomin feels the horizon to be just a little too wide. We prefer what is varying and capricious in a friendly way, what is unexpected and peculiar: the beach, which is partly ground and partly water; the sunset, which is partly dusk and partly light; and spring, which is partly cold and partly warm.

Now dusk fell again. It spread very slowly and carefully, to give the day ample time to go to bed. Small clouds were strewn all over the western sky like dabs of pink whipped cream. They were reflected on the ocean, which rested calm and smooth and looked quite harmless.

"Have you ever seen a cloud really close?" I asked Hodgkins.

"Yes," he answered. "In a book."

"I believe they are like blancmange," said the Joxter.

We sat chatting on a rock. The air was filled with

the tang of seaweed and of something else that might have been the smell of the ocean itself. I felt so happy that I wasn't even afraid it wouldn't last.

"Don't you feel good?" I asked.

"Rather," muttered Hodgkins and looked embarrassed (from that I knew he was exceedingly and enormously happy).

In that moment I caught sight of a whole flotilla of small boats putting out to sea. Light as butterflies, they went gliding away over their own reflections. All were manned by a silent crew: little grey-white beings huddling close together and staring out towards the horizon.

"Hattifatteners," Hodgkins said. "Electrical sailing."

"Hattifatteners," I whispered excitedly. "Travelling and travelling and never getting there . . ."

"Thunderstorms charge them," Hodgkins said. "Sting like nettles."

"And they live a wicked life," the Joxter informed.

"A wicked life?" I repeated with interest. "How?"

"I don't quite know," said the Joxter. "Trampling down people's gardens and drinking beer, and so on, I suppose."

We sat there for a long time looking after the Hattifatteners sailing out towards the horizon. I felt a strange desire to join them on their voyage and to share their wicked life. But I didn't say it.

"Well, and what about tomorrow?" asked the Joxter suddenly. "Do we put straight out to sea?"

Hodgkins looked at the *Oshun Oxtra.* "She's a river-boat," he said hesitatingly. "Paddle-wheels. No sails . . ."

"Let's toss," said the Joxter and got to his feet. "Muddler! Lend us a button, will you?"

The Muddler jumped out of the water and started to empty his pockets onto the rock.

"One's enough, dear nephew," said Hodgkins.

"Take your choice, folks!" said the Muddler happily. "Two or four holes? Bone, plush, wood, glass, metal, or mother-of-pearl? Single-coloured, mottled, speckled, spotted, striped, or chequered? Round, concave, convex, flat, octagonal, or—"

"Just a trouser button," said the Joxter. "Here goes. Right side up: we sail over the ocean. What's facing up?"

"The holes," said the Muddler, peering closely at the button in the dusk.

"Yes," I said. "But what else?"

Just then the Muddler whisked his whiskers, and the button disappeared in a crack.

"Excuse me! Dear me!" he exclaimed. "Here, have another."

"No," said the Joxter. "You can't toss more than once for anything. Now this matter has to settle itself, because I'm sleepy."

We had an unpleasant night aboard. When I was about to stretch out my legs in my bunk, the blanket was all sticky with some kind of treacly substance. The door-handles were sticky, too, and so were my toothbrush and my slippers, and Hodgkins's log-book simply wouldn't open at all.

"Nephew," he said, "you haven't done the cabin very well today."

"Excuse me!" cried the Muddler reproachfully. "I haven't done it at all!"

"My tobacco is all smeary," mumbled the Joxter, who liked to smoke in bed.

It was really very awkward. However, we calmed down and curled up in the least-sticky places. All night we were disturbed by strange noises that seemed to come from the pilot-house.

I awoke to an unusual and fateful clanging of the ship's bell.

"Get up! Get up! All hands on deck!" shouted the Muddler outside my door. "Water everywhere! So big! A lone, lone sea! And I left my best penwiper on the beach! My little penwiper's lying there all alone . . ."

We rushed on deck.

The *Oshun Oxtra* was splashing along over the sea, calmly and purposefully, and, I thought, with a certain secret delight.

Even unto this very day I have not been able to understand how two cog-wheels could bring about this movement, natural in a running river perhaps, but rather mysterious at sea. But every judgment tends to be vague, doesn't it? If a Hattifattener can be moved by its own electricity (which others call longing or unrest), then one shouldn't be astonished

if a boat manages with two cog-wheels. Well, I leave
this matter to the reader to ponder over, and return
to Hodgkins, who was looking with a frown at the
stump of his anchor-rope.

"Now I'm angry," he said. "Really and truly.
Angrier than ever before in my life. This rope has
been *gnawed.*"

We looked at each other.

"You know that my teeth are very small," I said.

"And I'm much too lazy to gnaw through a thick
rope like that," the Joxter observed.

"It wasn't me!" cried the Muddler, who never put
the blame on anybody. We always took him at his
word, because nobody had ever heard the Muddler
tell a fib, even about his collection (remarkably, because he was a true collector). I believe Muddlers
haven't the imagination.

Just then we heard a little cough behind us, and
when we turned around we saw a small Nibling
sitting under the sun tent.

"I see," said Hodgkins. *"I see,"* he said again,
with emphasis.

"I'm teething," the little Nibling explained shyly.
"I simply *had* to gnaw at something."

"But why the anchor-rope?" Hodgkins asked.

"It looked so old and worn I thought you
wouldn't mind," replied the Nibling.

"Why did you stow away, then?" I asked.

"I couldn't say," said the Nibling candidly. "I
sometimes have ideas I can't explain."

"And where did you hide?" the Joxter wondered.

The Nibling answered knowingly, "In your excellent Stevedoring Ltd. binnacle!" (Quite right; the binnacle was sticky, too.)

"Nibling," I said to end this surprising conversation, "what'll your mother say when she finds that you've run away?"

"She'll cry, I believe," said the Nibling.

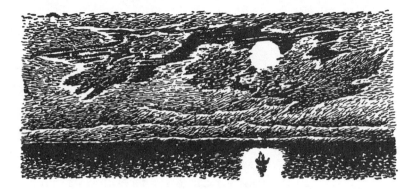

CHAPTER IV

In which the description of my ocean voyage culminates in a magnificent tempest and ends in a terrible surprise.

ight across the ocean ploughed the *Oshun Oxtra,* trailing her lonely wake. One day after another went bobbing by, each as sunny and sleepy and blue as the next. Schools of sea-spooks crossed our course, and now and then a giggling trail of mermaids appeared in our wake. We fed them oatmeal. Sometimes, when night drew closer over the sea, I liked to take over from Hodgkins at the helm. The moonlit deck that slowly rose and fell before me, the silence and the restless waves and clouds, and the solemn circle of the horizon—everything gave me the nice, exciting feeling of being terribly important and terribly small at the same time (perhaps, however, more the former).

Sometimes I could see the Joxter's pipe aglow in the dark when he came padding astern and sat down beside me.

"You'll have to admit that it's fun to do nothing at all," he said one night, and knocked the ashes from his pipe against the railing.

"Nothing at all?" I asked. "I'm steering. And you're smoking."

"Wherever you're steering us," said the Joxter.

"That's quite another matter," I replied, because even then I had a logical mind. "We were talking about doing things, not about what things we're doing. Are you having Forebodings again?" I added, worried.

"No." The Joxter yawned. "Hup, pff. It's all the same to me where we go. All places are all right. Good night, see you tomorrow."

"Cheerio," I replied.

When Hodgkins relieved me at dawn, I mentioned in passing the Joxter's strange and total lack of interest in his surroundings.

"Well," said Hodgkins, "perhaps he is really interested in everything, only he doesn't overdo it. For ourselves there is always one single interest. *You* want to become. *I* want to do. My nephew wants to have. But the Joxter just lives."

"Simply lives?" I said. "Anybody can do that."

"Mphm," Hodgkins said. Then he disappeared into his usual silence and a notebook in which he drew curious mechanical constructions that resembled cobwebs and bats.

Anyway, I think the Joxter's attitude a bit careless:

I mean, just to be living. Living is what you do anyway, isn't it? As I understand the question, you are surrounded all the time by lots of important things to be experienced or pondered over or conquered; there are so many possibilities that one's neck bristles rise when one tries to imagine them all —and in the midst of them I am sitting, and that's the really important thing, of course.

Now—today—I'm a bit worried by the fact that the opportunities aren't quite as many any more. I wonder why. In any case, I'm still sitting in their midst, and that's a consolation.

Later in the day the Muddler came up with the idea that we should send a wire to the Nibling's mother.

"No address. No telegraph office," said Hodgkins.

"Oh, of course," cried the Muddler. "How stupid of me! Excuse me!" And he crawled down into his tin again, somewhat embarrassed.

"What's a telegraph office?" asked the Nibling, who was sharing the Muddler's tin. "Can you eat it?"

"Don't ask me!" said the Muddler. "It's something big and intricate. It's where you send small signals to the other side of the earth . . . where they change into words!"

"How do you send them?" asked the Nibling.

"Through the air!" explained the Muddler vaguely and flapped his arms. "Not a single one gets lost on the way!"

"Dear me," said the Nibling, quite astonished.

After that he sat all the rest of the day craning his neck and looking for telegraph signals.

Around three o'clock the Nibling caught sight of a very large cloud. It came careening along very low, and it was chalk-white and woolly and looked quite unnatural.

"Picture-book cloud," observed Hodgkins.

"Have *you* read a picture-book?" I asked, surprised.

"Of course," he answered. "It was called *A Voyage over the Ocean.*"

The cloud went gliding past us to windward.

It stopped.

And suddenly something curious happened, not to mention uncanny: the cloud turned round and started to follow in our wake.

"Excuse me, but are clouds friendly?" asked the Muddler in a worried tone.

None of us could voice an opinion on that. The cloud came sailing along behind our ship; then it speeded up, rolled in over the rail, and softly thudded down on the deck, where it covered the Muddler's tin completely. Then it made itself comfortable, shook itself out from rail to rail, sagged a little —and I swear by my tail that the next moment this remarkable cloud had simply fallen asleep before our eyes!

"Have you ever seen anything like that?" I asked Hodgkins.

"Never," he replied decisively and disapprovingly.

The Nibling went up and chewed a little at the cloud, and declared that it tasted like his mother's pencil eraser at home.

"In any case it's soft," said the Joxter. He dug himself a suitable hole to sleep in, and the cloud at once closed itself around him like a friendly eiderdown. The cloud seemed to like us.

But navigation was very much hampered by this strange newcomer.

On the same day, just before sunset, the sky took on a curious look. It became yellow, not a friendly yellow but a dirty and eerie one. Over the horizon came marching a row of black clouds, frowning menacingly.

We were all of us sitting under the sun tent. The Muddler and the Nibling had succeeded in excavating their tin and had rolled it astern, where the deck was still cloudless.

The sea was rolling black and grey, and the sun grew hazy. The wind whistled anxiously in the stays. All the sea-spooks and mermaids had disappeared without a trace. We felt slightly worried.

Hodgkins gave me a look and said, "Moomin, check the aneroid barometer."

I crept ahead over our cloud and managed to force the door to the pilot-house open. Judge of my horror when I saw that the aneroid pointed to 670 —the lowest an aneroid barometer can point to!

I felt my nose become stiff with suspense, and thought, "I believe I'm turning pale . . . white as a sheet or ashen grey. How interesting." I crawled quickly back astern and shouted, "Do you see that I'm white as a sheet?"

"I dare say you're looking the same as usual," said the Joxter. "What did it show?"

"670," I replied, slightly hurt, as you can imagine.

It has often astounded me that the dramatic heights in one's life are so often spoiled by the trivial, almost disparaging observations of others. Even if these aren't uttered out of spite, one can't deny that there is great thoughtlessness behind them. In my opinion, one should always make the most out of an awful situation, partly because of the local colour I have mentioned earlier, partly because one's fright is to some degree diminished if one enlarges the fright-fulness. Besides that, it is great fun to make an impression. Thoughts like these, of course, are not for Joxters to comprehend. But the gift of understanding others is unevenly distributed, and who am I to doubt the mysterious mission even of a Joxter.

However, Hodgkins wriggled his ears and turned his nose to the wind. He looked with loving care at the *Oshun Oxtra.* Then he said, "She's well built.

She'll manage. The Muddler and the Nibling are to keep in their tin and put the lid on, because we're in for a gale."

"Have you been in a gale before?" I asked cautiously.

"Certainly," replied Hodgkins. "In the picture-book *A Voyage over the Ocean.* No waves can be bigger than those."

And then the gale was upon us, suddenly, like all real gales. The *Oshun Oxtra* nearly lost her balance in the first surprise, but soon this splendid river-boat was abreast of the situation and splashed along as well as she could for the rage of the elements.

The sun tent was torn away like a leaf and flapped out to sea (it was a nice sun tent. I hope somebody found it and enjoyed it). The Muddler's tin had rolled and stuck under the railing, and every time the *Oshun Oxtra* took a dive or was lifted high on a wave-crest all his buttons, suspenders, tin-openers,

nails, and glass pearls made a terrible clatter inside. The Muddler cried that he was feeling sick, but there wasn't anything we could do about that. We could only cling to the holds we found, staring horror-struck out over the darkening ocean.

The sun was gone. The horizon was gone. All was different, strange, and inimical. Hissing specks of white foam from the waves were flying past us, and beyond the railing everything was black, inconceivable chaos. Suddenly I understood with blighting insight that I didn't know anything about the sea or about ships. I called out for Hodgkins, but he didn't hear me. I was totally alone and deserted, and it was of no help to be in the midst of an unquestionably Highly Dramatical happening. I felt no desire at all to enlarge the frightfulness; on the contrary, dear reader! Perhaps one makes the most out of an awful situation only when one has onlookers? I decided quickly to make less of it instead. I thought, "Now, if I close my eyes and pretend that I'm nobody at all and that no one remembers my existence, perhaps all this will go away . . . As a matter of fact, it's nothing at all to do with me! I'm here quite by mistake . . ." And I closed my eyes and made myself small and said over and over, "Never mind. I'm quite small. I'm sitting in the Hemulen's garden hammock, and I'll be going inside to eat porridge in a little while . . ."

"Moomin!" Hodgkins shouted through the gale. "They're smaller!"

I didn't understand.

"Smaller!" he cried. "Much smaller waves than in the picture-book!"

But I had never seen the waves in Hodgkins's picture-book, so I shut my eyes, as before, and took a firm hold of the Hemulen's garden hammock. It helped. In a little while I really could feel the hammock quietly rocking back and forth. The gale subsided and nothing felt perilous any more. So I opened my eyes and saw an unbelievable sight. The *Oshun Oxtra* was floating along on high, carried forward by a great white sail. Far below us the gale continued among black, heaving seas. Only now it looked like a little toy gale that didn't concern us.

"We're flying! We're flying!" cried Hodgkins. He was standing beside me at the rail and staring at the cloud up in our rigging, like a large white balloon.

"How did you get it up there?" I asked.

"It rigged itself," he replied. "A flying river-boat . . . !" And he sank into thought.

The night slowly paled towards dawn. The sky turned grey, and it was very cold. By and by I forgot that I had tried to hide in the Hemulen's garden hammock. I felt secure and curious again and began to think of coffee. It was really terribly cold. I carefully shook my paws and examined my tail and ears. Nothing was injured by the gale.

The Joxter was there, too. He was sitting next to the Muddler's tin, trying to light his pipe.

But the *Oshun Oxtra* was in a sorry shape. The mast was broken, the paddles gone. Torn stays dangled sadly, and the rails were smashed in several places. The deck was strewn with flotsam, seaweed, and here and there an unconscious sea-spook. Worst of all, the gilt knob had disappeared from the roof of the pilot-house.

Slowly our cloud tired, and the river-boat sank down towards the sea. When the sky reddened in the east, we were rolling in the long swells after the gale, and I heard the buttons rattling in the Muddler's tin. The white picture-book cloud had fallen asleep between the rails again.

"Dear crew," Hodgkins said solemnly, "we have ridden out the gale. Let my nephew out, please!"

We prised off the lid, and the Muddler appeared, pitifully green in the face.

"Mother of all buttons," he said wearily, "what have I done to be so sick? Oh, what a life, what troubles, what worries . . . Just *look* at my collection! Oh, fate!"

The Nibling came out also, sniffed the wind, and snorted. Then he said, "I'm hungry."

"Excuse me," cried the Muddler. "Even to *think* of food makes me—"

"Easy now," I said. "I'll make some coffee."

When I went forward I looked boldly at the sea over the broken railing and thought, "Now I know quite a lot about you! And about ships! And clouds! Next time I'm not going to shut my eyes and make myself small!"

When the coffee was ready, the sun rose over the world. Mild and friendly, it shone on my cold stomach and revived my courage. I remembered how it had risen my first day of freedom after the historic escape, and how it shone that morning I built a house in the sand. I'm born in August under the proud signs of the Lion and the Sun, preordained to follow the adventurous path that my stars determine.

Gales, well! Their purpose is most likely to provide a sunrise afterwards. The pilot-house would get a new gilt knob. I drank my coffee contentedly.

Now a page was turned, and I was nearing a new chapter of my life. There was land ahead, a large lonely island in the middle of the sea! The proud silhouette of an unknown coast!

I stood on my head and shouted, "Hodgkins! Something's happening again!"

The Muddler at once stopped being sick and started to put his tin in order for landing. The Nibling chewed at his own tail from pure nervousness, and Hodgkins set me to polishing all the remaining brass-work. (The Joxter did nothing at all.) We were drifting straight on to the foreign coast. High on a hill we could see something that looked like a light-house. This tower was slowly moving, as if reaching around—rather an astounding phenomenon. But we were too busy to worry about it.

When the *Oshun Oxtra* glided towards the shore, we gathered together by the railing, newly combed, and with tails and teeth brushed.

That was when we heard a thundering voice somewhere high above us, and the following fright-

ful words: "Ha! I'm groked if this isn't Hodgkins and
his begreebled gang! At last I've got you!"

Surprise! It was Edward the Booble, and he was
horrifyingly angry.

*"That's how life was when I was young!" said
Moominpappa, and closed his book.*

*"Read some more, please!" cried Sniff. "What
happened then? Did the Booble try to tread on you?"*

*"Next time," Moominpappa said with an air of
mystery. "That was thrilling, eh? But you see, it's a
trick all good authors use, to close a chapter at the
ghastliest moment."*

*This time Moominpappa was sitting on the sandy
beach with his son, Snufkin, and Sniff. When he read
to them about the terrible gale, they gazed out over the
sea, which rolled little rippling waves on to the beach.*

They imagined the Oshun Oxtra *careering along
like a ghost ship through the gale, manned by their
fathers.*

*"How sick he must have been in his tin," mumbled
Sniff.*

*"It's cold here," said Moominpappa. "Let's take
a walk."*

*They wandered off over the dried seaweed towards
the point.*

"Can you imitate a Nibling?" asked Snufkin.

*Moominpappa tried. "No-o," he said. "It didn't
come out right. It should sound as if it came through
a tin tube."*

*"It wasn't so far off," said Moomintroll. "Father,
didn't you go away with the Hattifatteners later on?"*

"Well," answered Moominpappa in some embarrassment, "perhaps I did. But that was very, very much later. I think it won't come into the book at all."

"I think it should!" cried Sniff. "Did you live a wicked life with them?"

"Shut up!" said Moomintroll.

"Dash, dash, dash," said Moominpappa. "Look, there's something that's floated ashore! Run along and see what it is!"

They ran off.

"What can that be?" said Snufkin. It was a heavy, onion-shaped thing. It seemed to have floated around for a very long time, because it was covered with weeds and barnacles. In a few places there were some traces of gold paint on the cracked wood.

Moominpappa lifted the wooden onion in his paws and looked closely at it. And as he looked, his eyes grew larger and larger, and finally he covered them with one paw and sighed.

"Children," he said solemnly and a little shakily,

"what you behold here is the knob from the roof of the pilot-house of the Oshun Oxtra!*"*

"Oh," said Moomintroll, *with great awe.*

"And now," continued Moominpappa, *overcome by his memories, "now I'm going to start on an important new chapter and contemplate this unique discovery in solitude. Run along and play in the cave!"*

Moominpappa walked along to the point with the golden knob under one arm and his Memoirs under the other.

"I really was a strapping Moomin in my day," he said to himself. *"And still going strong!"* he added, and stamped his feet with a happy smile.

CHAPTER V

*In which (after giving a small specimen of my intel-
lectual powers) I describe the Mymble family and the
great Surprise Party that brought me some fascinating tokens of honour from the paw of the Autocrat.*

I am to this day firmly convinced that Edward the Booble had intended to sit down
on us. Doubtless he would have wept bit-
terly afterwards and tried to console his
conscience by arranging a very beautiful
funeral. And most certainly he would have forgotten
the sad incident very quickly and gone off and sat
down on someone else he happened to dislike.

Be that as it may, at the moment of decision I had
an idea. There was a "click," as usual, and the idea
emerged. I advanced fearlessly on that mountain of
rage and said with a studied calm, "Hello, Uncle!
Glad to see you again. Are your feet still sore?"

"You have the nerve to ask me that?" roared

81

Edward the Booble. "You water-flea! *Yes,* my feet are sore! *Yes,* my behind is sore, too! And that's because of you!"

"Well, in that case," I replied in a perfectly controlled voice, "in that case, the present we've brought you will suit you all the better: a genuine eider-down Booble Sleeping-Bag! Especially made for Boobles that have sat themselves on something and need a bit of comfort!"

"Sleeping-bag? Eider-down?" Edward the Booble said and peered near-sightedly at our cloud. "You're deceiving me again, you grokely dishrags. I suppose that pillow is stuffed with rocks . . ." He pulled the cloud ashore and sniffed suspiciously at it.

"Sit down, Edward, won't you! Nice and soft!"

"I've heard that before," said the Booble. "Nice and soft, you said. And what happened? The prickliest, hardest, pestilentiallest, stoniest, knobbliest, grokely ruggedest . . ." And Edward the Booble sank down on the cloud and became thoughtfully silent.

"Well?" we cried expectantly.

"Hrrumph," said the Booble sourly. "There seem to be a few softer spots. I'll sit here and think for a while until I've decided whether to begreeble you or not."

But when Edward the Booble reached his decision we were far away from that fatal place that so easily might have become the scene of the end of all my dreams and hopes.

★   ★   ★

Happily arrived deep in the strange and foreign country, we mostly beheld round, grassy hills in every direction. It seemed to be a country of rounded knolls, and up and down these green slopes there ran miles of low stone walls, long and innumerable, no mean output of work by somebody. But the few and scattered houses were mostly built of straw, quite carelessly, in my opinion.

"Why have they built all these walls?" the Joxter wondered. "Are they shutting someone in or are they to shut us out? And where is everybody, by the way?"

All was quite silent. There was not a trace of the excited crowd that should have come running to take interest in us and our gale and to admire us and feel sorry for us. I was very disappointed and I'm sure the others shared my feelings. However, as we passed a small house that was—if possible—still more carelessly built than the other ones, we heard from within it the unmistakable sound of someone playing on a comb. We knocked four times, but no one answered the door.

"Hello! Ahoy!" Hodgkins shouted. "Anybody home?"

Then we heard a small voice that answered, "No, no! Nobody at all!"

"That's funny," I said. "Then who's talking?"

"I'm the Mymble's daughter," said the voice. "But you'll have to go away quick-quick, because I'm not allowed to open the door to anybody until Mother comes back."

"Where's Mother, then?" asked Hodgkins.

"She's at a garden party," the little voice answered sadly.

"Well, why didn't she take you along?" the Muddler asked in a shocked voice. "Are you too small?"

At that the Mymble's daughter started to sob and said, "I've a sore throat today! Mother thinks it's diphtheria!"

"Open the door, won't you?" Hodgkins said kindly. "We'll have a look at your throat. Don't be afraid."

The Mymble's daughter opened the door. She had a woollen scarf around her neck, and her eyes were quite red.

"Let's see now," Hodgkins said. "Open your mouth. Say a-a-a-ah!"

"Mother also thought it could be typhoid fever or cholera," mumbled the Mymble's daughter sadly. "A-a-a-ah!"

"Not a spot," Hodgkins said. "Does it hurt?"

"Terribly," groaned the Mymble's daughter. "I think my throat's growing together, so I'll not be able to breathe, or eat or talk, either."

"You'll have to go to bed at once," Hodgkins said. "We'll find your mother for you. Immediately!"

"No, no, please don't," exclaimed the Mymble's daughter. "Really, I just fibbed. I'm not ill at all. Mother left me at home because I've been so impossible that even she got tired of me."

"Fibbed? Whatever for?" Hodgkins asked in astonishment.

"To have a little fun!" said the Mymble's daugh-

ter, and started to wail once more. "I've nothing on earth to do!"

"Can't we take her along and go to that garden party?" the Joxter proposed.

"Perhaps the Mymble wouldn't like it," I said.

"Of course she would!" said her daughter happily. "Mamma loves foreigners! And she's sure to have forgotten how impossible I am. She forgets everything!"

The little Mymble took off her woolly scarf and

rushed out. "Hurry up!" she shouted. "The King must have started his Surprises long ago."

"The King!" I exclaimed. There was a hollow feeling in my stomach. "Do you mean a real King?"

"Real?" repeated the Mymble's daughter. "Indeed he's real! He's an Autocrat and the greatest King alive! And today is his birthday—he's a hundred years old today!"

"Does he resemble me?" I whispered.

"No, not in the least," said the Mymble's daughter in astonishment. "Why on earth should he resemble you?"

I mumbled something vague and felt my face redden. Of course, it had been a rash idea. But still. It might still . . . I *felt* royal. Oh, well. In any case, I was going to see an Autocrat, perhaps even speak to him!

Kings are something truly special; there is something dignified, elevated, unreachable about them. In general I'm not apt to admire people (Hodgkins possibly excepted). But you can admire a King without feeling too small yourself. That's a nice feeling.

The Mymble's daughter was trotting away at great speed ahead of us, jumping over a stone wall now and then.

"Tell me," said the Joxter, "why are all these walls here? Are you shutting people in or out?"

"Oh, they have no special meaning," answered the Mymble's daughter. "The subjects think it's fun to build them, because then you can take your food along with you and have a picnic. My maternal uncle has built ten miles of them! You'd be surprised at my uncle," she continued happily. "He studies letters and words from all sides and likes to walk around them until he's quite sure of them. It takes him hours and hours to do the longest words!"

"Like 'otolaryngologist,' " said the Joxter.

"Or 'kalospinterochromatokrene,' " I said.

"Oh," said the Mymble's daughter, "if they're *that* long, he has to camp beside them. At night he sleeps in his long red beard. Half the beard's his cover and the other half's his mattress. In the daytime he keeps two small white mice in it, and they're so sweet they don't have to pay any rent."

"Excuse me, but I believe she's fibbing again," said the Muddler.

"That's what my brothers and sisters believe, too," said the Mymble's daughter. "There are fourteen or fifteen of them, and they all think the same. I'm the oldest and wisest. Well, here we are. Remember to tell Mamma that you coaxed me to come with you."

"What does she look like?" asked the Joxter.

"She's round," said the Mymble's daughter. "Everything about her's round. Probably inside her, too."

We were standing before a gate, festooned with flowers, set in an exceptionally high stone wall. Above it was a large placard reading:

The Autocrat's Garden Party
FREE FOR ALL!
Come in, come in, please!
The Surprise Party of the Year
Very Special!
(Because of the 100th Anniversary of Our Birth)
DON'T BE AFRAID
if Anything Happens!

"What will happen?" asked the Nibling.

"Anything," said the Mymble's daughter. "That's what's so thrilling."

We went into the garden. It was wild and overgrown in a kind of careless and good-natured way.

"Excuse me, are there any wild beasts?" asked the Muddler.

"Much worse," whispered the Mymble's daughter. "Five hundred percent of the guests simply disappear! It's unspeakable. I'll run along now. See you later."

We walked carefully. A long tunnel filled with a green and mysterious light led us through the thickets and bushes.

"Stop!" cried Hodgkins with his ears all cocked.

An abyss yawned before us! And down there (no, it's really almost too frightful to mention) crouched a hairy and goggling Thing, on long, quivering legs—a giant spider!

"Hush, hush! Let's see if he's angry," whispered the Joxter and threw a couple of pebbles. The spider wobbled his legs, swayed horribly, and cast his eyes about (they were on stalks).

"Artificial," Hodgkins remarked with interest. "Legs of wire springs. Good work."

"Excuse me, but I don't think it's right to play jokes like that," said the Muddler. "As if one weren't afraid enough of *really* dangerous things!"

"Foreigners," said Hodgkins in an explanatory way and shrugged his shoulders.

I felt much shaken, not so much by the Autocrat's spider as by his other-than-Regal behaviour.

At the next turning was hung a placard with large, hilarious letters:

SCARED—WEREN'T YOU!

How can a King want to be so childish, I thought, feeling a bit upset. It's unworthy—especially if the King is a hundred years old! One should be careful of one's subjects' respect and admiration.

After a while we reached an artificial lake and looked at it with some suspicion.

Small, brightly painted dinghies bearing the Autocratical colours lay by the beach. Friendly-looking trees were leaning out over the water.

"I don't quite believe it," mumbled the Joxter and stepped into a bright red boat with an azure rail.

We were out in the middle of the lake before the

King launched his next surprise. A strong jet of water shot up beside our boat and drenched us to the skin. The Muddler screamed with understandable fright. Before we reached the other beach we had four more showers, and on the shore we found another placard asking us:

WET—AREN'T YOU?

I felt quite bewildered, and embarrassed on behalf of the King.

"Funny kind of garden party," mumbled Hodgkins.

"I like it!" cried the Joxter. "The Autocrat must be a jolly person. He doesn't take himself one bit in earnest!"

I gave the Joxter a look but controlled myself.

We came to a whole network of canals with a maze of bridges. The bridges were broken or craftily mended with cardboard, and at times we had to cross balancing on rotten tree-trunks or on bridges suspended on old strings and rope-ends. But nothing special happened, except that the Nibling dived head first into a mud-bank and really seemed quite enlivened by this.

Suddenly the Joxter exclaimed, "Aha! This time he won't pull *my* leg." And he walked straight up to a big stuffed bull and gave it a smack on the muzzle. Judge of our fright when the bull gave a terrific bellow, lowered its horns (luckily, they were padded), and sent the Joxter in a splendid arc straight into a rose-bush.

And of course we found another placard triumphantly teasing us:

DIDN'T THINK IT WOULD—DID YOU?

This time I thought that the Autocrat showed a sense of humour, of a kind.

By and by we became accustomed to the Surprises. We went wandering farther and farther, deeper and deeper into the King's tangled garden, passing leafy caverns and secret hiding places of every sort, under waterfalls and over new abysses illuminated with Bengal lights. And the Autocrat had provided his guests with things other than trapdoors, explosions, and wire-spring monsters. If you looked carefully at the roots of bushes, in hollow trees, and in cracks in the rocks, you sometimes found small nests containing one or more brightly coloured or golden eggs. Each egg was beautifully painted with a number. I found numbers 67, 14, 890, 223, and 27. It was the Autocrat's Royal Lottery. Generally speaking, I don't like games and contests, because I get so very crestfallen if I don't win, but I liked hunting for these eggs. The Nibling found the most, and it was hard to make him understand that they weren't to be eaten but instead should be saved for the draw. Hodgkins came a good second, then I, and finally the Joxter—who was too lazy to search in earnest—and the Muddler, whose only method was hopping around.

Finally we discovered a long, gaudy ribbon that

was slung between the trees and tied in bows. A large placard told us:

THIS IS WHERE THE REAL FUN STARTS!

We heard happy whoops, bangs, and music; the party was in full swing in the middle of the garden.

"I think I'll stay here and wait for you," said the Nibling a little nervously. "It sounds a bit disorderly!"

"As you like," said Hodgkins. "Only don't get lost."

We stopped at the outskirts of a great open meadow that was filled with subjects of the Autocrat —riding on roller-coasters, shouting, singing, throwing squibs at each other, and eating spun sugar. In the middle stood a large circular house that played music and whirled around with fluttering pennants, and thronged with white horses in silver harness.

"What's that?" I cried, enraptured.

"A merry-go-round," Hodgkins replied. "I drew the machinery for you. In cross section. Don't you remember?"

"It didn't look like this at all," I protested. "This one is all horses and silver and pennants and music!"

"*And* cog-wheels," said Hodgkins.

"Ginger ale, please?" asked a big Hemulen in a definitely unbecoming pinafore (I've always said so: Hemulens have no taste). She gave us a glass each and said importantly, "Now you're to go and wish the Autocrat many happy returns of the day. It's his hundredth birthday, you know."

I took my glass of ginger ale with mixed feelings and raised my eyes towards the Autocrat's throne. There he sat, all wrinkly, and not resembling me a bit. Was that disappointment I felt—or was it relief? To look up towards a Throne is a solemn and important moment. Every Moomin must have something to look up to (and to look down on, of course), something that awakes veneration and noble feelings. Well, what I saw was a King with his crown askew and flowers behind his ears, a King who was banging his knees and stamping his feet in time to the music so that his throne wobbled! Under it he kept a fog-horn and gave a short blast every time he wished to acknowledge a toast from any of his subjects. Need I say that I felt terribly embarrassed and dejected?

In a pause when the fog-horn was silent, Hodgkins said, "Many happy returns of the century!"

I saluted with my tail and said in an unnatural voice, "Your Autocratical Majesty, permit a refugee from a far-off coast to convey his good wishes. This is a moment suited to many reflections!"

The King stared at me in surprise and started to giggle.

"Cheerio!" he said. "Did you get wet? What did the bull say? Don't tell me that no one fell in the treacle trap! Oh, what fun it is to be King!"

Then the King tired of us and started his fog-horn. "Hello, my people good and true!" he cried. "(Stop that merry-go-round, somebody.) Come hither, all! It's time to draw the lottery prizes!"

The merry-go-round and the swings stopped, and everybody came running with their eggs.

"701!" shouted the King. "Who's got number 701?"

"I have," said Hodgkins.

"Here you are, please! Have a good time," said the Autocrat and handed him an exceedingly neat fret-saw of the kind he had always wanted. New winning numbers were called, and the subjects formed a long line before the throne, laughing and babbling. Every single Creep and Toffle seemed to have won something, but not I.

The Joxter and the Muddler had arranged their winnings before them and were now making short work of them, because most of their prizes were chocolate balls, marzipan Hemulens, and spun-sugar roses. Hodgkins, however, was sitting with a heap of practical and uninteresting things in his lap, mostly tools.

Finally the Autocrat clambered up to stand on his throne and cried, "My dear people! Dear muddle-headed, fuzzy, and thoughtless subjects! Each of you has won exactly the things that suit him best, and no more than he has earned. In Our centennial wisdom We have hidden the eggs in three kinds of places. First, where you might stumble on them when running about or being too lazy to look carefully: all those prizes are eatable. Second, We have hidden some eggs where they can be found with meticulous and methodical search: those prizes are useful. And third, We have chosen hiding places that need some

imagination to find: those prizes are of no use whatever. Now, my pig-headed, dear, and silly subjects!
Who of you have looked in fancy places: under
stones, in the brooks, in the tree-tops, in flower-buds,
in his own pockets, or in ant hills? Who has found
numbers 67, 14, 890, 999, 223, and 27?"

"I have," I shouted, so loudly that I jumped high
with embarrassment. And shortly after me a smaller
voice beside me said, "999!"

"Come hither, poor Moomin," said the Autocrat. "Behold the utterly useless rewards of a fantastical imagination. Do you like them?"

"Terribly, Your Majesty," I breathed, enchantedly looking at my prizes. I think 27 was the nicest. It was a drawing-room decoration: a small meerschaum tram on a coral pedestal. The center was designed as a small box to keep safety pins in. Number 67 was a champagne whisk set with garnets. The other prizes were a shark's tooth, a preserved smoking-ring, and a decorated barrel-organ crank. Can you understand my bliss? And can you understand, dear Reader, that I almost forgave the Autocrat for not being as Regal as he should have been, and all at once thought him a rather pleasant King?

"And what about me?" cried the Mymble's daughter (it was of course she who had number 999).

"Little Mymble," said the Autocrat gravely, "you are entitled to kiss Us on Our nose."

The Mymble's daughter climbed on to the Autocrat's lap and kissed him on his old Autocratic nose. The multitude cheered madly and started eating their prizes.

It was a garden party of sumptuous proportions. At dusk, coloured lanterns were lighted all over the Garden of Surprises. Dancing started, happy fights broke out, the Autocrat distributed balloons and opened large vats of apple wine, and by innumerable camp-fires the subjects were cooking soup and grilling sausages. I was milling around with the others when I perceived a large Mymble who seemed wholly built of circles and arcs. I went up to her, bowed, and asked, "Excuse me, madam, do you happen to be the Mymble?"

"Herself!" said the Mymble, laughing. "Tumble and bumble, what lots I've eaten! Moomin, weren't you sorry to get such peculiar prizes?"

"Peculiar?" I exclaimed. "Can you win anything better than the useless rewards of a fantastical imagination! Is there any greater honour?" Politely I added, "And of course, your daughter won the main prize."

"She's a credit to the family," the Mymble conceded proudly.

"So you're not angry with her any more?" I asked.

"Angry?" said the Mymble, surprised. "Why should I be? I haven't the time to be angry. Eighteen, nineteen kiddies to wash, put to bed, button up and button down, feed, wipe the nose of, and the Groke knows what. No, young friend, I'm enjoying myself all the time!"

"And what a singular brother you have," I continued by way of conversation.

"Brother?" said the Mymble.

"Yes, your daughter's maternal uncle," I explained. "Who sleeps in his long red beard." (Luckily, I said nothing about those mice that were living in his beard.)

At this the Mymble laughed at the top of her voice and said, "What a daughter I have indeed! She's been pulling your leg, Moomin! She hasn't any uncle that I know of. Cheerio—I'm going to try the

merry-go-round!" And the Mymble collected as many of her children as her broad lap could hold and climbed into a red carriage drawn by a dapple-grey horse.

"What a remarkable Mymble," said the Joxter with sincere admiration.

On a horse the Muddler sat, looking quaint.

"How's it going?" I asked. "Isn't it fun?"

"Yes, thanks, splendid," mumbled the Muddler. "I'm really having a good time. But this going round and round makes you a bit sick in the end . . . It's a pity!"

"How many times have you ridden this?" I asked.

"Don't know," replied the Muddler faintly. "A lot! Such a lot! Excuse me, but I have to! This may be the only time in my life I ride a merry-go-round . . . Oh, here we go again!"

"Time to go home," said Hodgkins. "Where's the King?"

But the Autocrat was busy at the roller-coaster, so we left discreetly. Only the Joxter stayed. He explained that the Mymble and he were going to swing on the swings until sunrise.

At the outskirts of the meadow we found our Nibling, who had dug himself a hole in the moss and gone to sleep.

"Hello," I said. "Haven't you claimed your prizes?"

"Prizes?" said the Nibling and blinked his eyes.

"Your eggs," said Hodgkins. "You had a dozen."

"I ate them," answered the Nibling shyly. "I hadn't anything else to do while I waited for you."

I've often wondered what the Nibling's prizes would have been, and who got them when he didn't ask for them. Perhaps the Autocrat saved them for his next centennial party.

Moominpappa turned a page. "Chapter six," he said.

"Just a moment," Snufkin said. "Did my father like this Mymble?"

"Did he indeed!" replied Moominpappa. "They were always running around together and laughing,

whether there was anything to laugh at or not, as far
as I can remember."

"Did he like her more than me?" asked Snufkin.

"But you didn't exist yet," said Moominpappa.

Snufkin snorted. He pulled his hat down over his
ears and looked out of the window.

Moominpappa gave him a look. Then he arose and
padded off to the cabinet in the corner, where he poked
about on the upper shelf for quite a time. When he
returned he held a long, shining shark's tooth. "This
is for you," he said. "Your father used to admire it."

Snufkin looked at the shark's tooth. "It's fine," he
said. "I'll hang it over my bed. Did he get hurt when
the bull threw him in the rose-bush?"

"No!" said Moominpappa. "The Joxter was as
supple as a cat, and the bull had padded horns."

"Well, and what became of the other prizes?"
asked Sniff. "The tram is down there by the drawing-
room mirror, but where are the other ones?"

"Well, we never had any champagne," Moominpappa mused. "So I suppose the whisk is still in the
back of the kitchen drawer. And the smoke-ring
evaporated with the years . . ."

"But the decorated barrel-organ crank!" Sniff
shouted.

"Oh, yes," said Moominpappa. "If I only knew
when your birthday came along . . . But your daddy
always muddled his dates."

"My name-day, then!" entreated Sniff.

"Good, you'll get a mysterious present on your next
name-day," said Moominpappa. "Quiet now, so I
can read you some more."

CHAPTER VI

*In which I found a colony, suffer a crisis, and call
forth the Ghost of Horror Island.*

hall I soon forget the morning Hodgkins
received an urgent telegram? It began
peacefully and nicely. We were all sitting
in the pilot-house of the *Oshun Oxtra,*
drinking coffee.

"I want some coffee, too," said the Nibling and
blew bubbles in his glass of milk.

"You're too little," Hodgkins explained kindly.
"And as it happens, you're being sent home to
your mother. On the packet-boat, in half an
hour."

"You don't say," replied the Nibling calmly, and
continued bubbling his milk.

"But I'm staying with you!" cried the Mymble's

daughter. "Until I'm grown up. Listen, Hodgkins, can't you invent something to make Mymbles really terribly big?"

"A small Mymble is enough," I said.

"That's what Mother says, too," she admitted. "Do you know that I was brought into the world in a cockle-shell, and I was no bigger than a water-flea when she found me in her aquarium?"

"You're fibbing again," I said. "I know perfectly well that people grow inside their mothers, just like pips in an apple! And one can't have Mymbles aboard a ship, it's unlucky."

"Balderdash," said the Mymble's daughter carelessly, and swallowed some more coffee.

We tied an address tag on the Nibling's tail and kissed him on the nose. To his great credit, he didn't bite a single one of us.

"Give our regards to your mother," Hodgkins said. "And don't tear the packet-boat to pieces."

"No, no," the Nibling promised happily. And so off he went in the company of the Mymble's daughter, who was to make sure that he got on board.

Hodgkins spread a map of the world on the table of the pilot-house. And at that moment there was a knock on the door, and a thundering voice shouted, "Telegram! Urgent telegram for Mr. Hodgkins!" Outside the door stood a big Hemulen of the Royal Autocratic Guards. Hodgkins calmly put on his captain's cap and looked at his telegram with a serious frown. It read as follows:

OUR ATTENTION DIRECTED FACT HODG-
KINS FIRSTCLASS INVENTOR STOP PLEASE
PLACE TALENTS AUTOCRATS SERVICE EX-
CLAMATION MARK URGENT

"Excuse me, but he doesn't seem to be any grand letter-writer, this King," said the Muddler, who had taught himself to read with the help of his coffee tin ("Maxwell House Coffee High Grade One Pound," and so forth) while it was still blue, of course.

"That's how urgent telegrams are," explained Hodgkins. "No time to put in all the words. On the contrary, a very fine telegram."

He had found his hairbrush behind the binnacle and was now grooming his ears. Tufts of hair were flying all over the cabin.

"May I put in the small words in your fine telegram?" asked the Muddler.

Hodgkins didn't listen. He mumbled something and started brushing his trousers.

"Hodgkins," I said cautiously. "If you're going to invent things for the Autocrat, then we can't do any travelling, can we?"

Hodgkins made an absentminded sound.

"And inventions take a long time, don't they?" I continued.

As Hodgkins didn't answer me, I cried in full desperation, "How can you be an adventurer if you live in the same place all the time? Don't you *want* to be an adventurer?"

But Hodgkins replied, "No. I want to be an inventor. I want to invent a flying river-boat."

"And what about me?" I asked.

"Why don't you found a colony with the others?" Hodgkins replied kindly, and left.

That same afternoon, Hodgkins moved into the Garden of Surprises, and he took the *Oshun Oxtra* with him. Only the pilot-house was left by itself on the shore. The Autocratic Guards rolled the riverboat up to the pleasure-ground and surrounded it with the utmost secrecy and eight stone walls, which the subjects built enthusiastically.

Cartloads of tools were rolled inside, tons of cogwheels, and miles of wire springs. Hodgkins promised the Autocrat to spend his Tuesdays and Thursdays inventing funny things with which to scare the subjects. Otherwise he was given a free paw to construct his flying river-boat. All this I heard about afterwards. At the time I only felt abandoned. I began to mistrust the Autocrat again, and did not feel able to admire Kings. And I didn't have the least idea of what was meant by the strange word "colony." At last I went to the Mymble's house to be comforted.

"Hello," said the Mymble's daughter, who was standing at the pump washing her small sisters and brothers. "You look as if you've eaten raw cranberries!"

"I'm not an adventurer any more. I'm going to found a colony," I replied glumly.

"Indeed. And what's that?" asked the Mymble's daughter.

"I don't know," I mumbled. "Probably something very silly. I believe I'd better be off to join the

Hattifatteners, lonely as the desert wind or the eagle of the oceans."

"I'll come along with you," declared the Mymble's daughter, and stopped pumping.

"There's a lot of difference between Hodgkins and you," I said in a tone that wholly missed its intended effect.

"Indeed there is!" she cried happily. "Mother! Where are you? Where's she gone off now?"

"Hello," said the Mymble from behind a bush. "How many have you washed?"

"Half," replied her daughter. "I'm leaving the rest because this Moomin has asked me along on a tour round the world, lonely as the desert wind or the chaffinch!"

"No, no, no!" I exclaimed with understandable alarm. "It wasn't like that at all!"

"Well, as the eagle of the oceans, then," said the Mymble's daughter.

But her mother cried in surprise, "You don't say! So you won't be home for dinner?"

"Oh, Mother," said the Mymble's daughter. "Next time you see me, I'll be the biggest Mymble in the world! Are we starting at once?"

"On second thought, perhaps a colony would be better," I said faintly.

"Fine," she replied happily. "We're colonists, then! Look, Mother, I'm a real colonist, and now I'm moving from home!"

Dear reader, for your own well-being I beg of you to be most careful with Mymbles. They are interested in anything and can't ever understand that you're not interested in them.

Thus, against my own wish, I founded a colony together with the Mymble's daughter, the Muddler, and the Joxter. We met in Hodgkins's abandoned pilot-house.

"Well," said the Mymble's daughter, "now I've asked Mother what colonists are, and she thought they're people living as close to each other as possible because they very much dislike being alone. And then they start quarrelling terribly because anyway that's more fun than having nobody at all to quarrel with! Mother warned me."

Her words were followed by a disapproving silence.

"Must we start quarrelling now?" asked the Muddler anxiously. "I dislike quarrels very much! Excuse me, quarrels are so sad!"

"That was quite wrong!" cried the Joxter. "A

colony is a place where you live in peace and quiet as far away as possible from other people. Now and then something unusual happens, and afterwards there's peace and quiet again . . . You can live in an apple tree, for instance. Songs and sunshine and sleeping in every morning, if you see what I mean. Nobody jumping about and telling you that there are important things that can't be put off . . . You let them take care of themselves!"

"And do they take care of themselves?" asked the Muddler.

"Of course," said the Joxter dreamily. "You just leave them alone. The oranges grow and the flowers open, and now and then some new Joxter is born to eat them and smell them. And the sun shines on it all."

"No! That's no colony!" I cried. "I believe a colony is a society of outlaws! A society doing things that are terribly adventurous and a little frightening, things that nobody else dares."

"Such as what?" asked the Mymble's daughter, interested.

"You'll see," I replied mysteriously. "By midnight next Friday! You'll be surprised!"

The Muddler cheered. The Mymble's daughter clapped her paws.

But the dismal truth was that I didn't have the least idea of what to invent for them by midnight the coming Friday.

We at once adopted total independence.

The Joxter moved into an apple tree near the

Mymble's house. The Mymble's daughter declared
that she was going to sleep in a new place every
night in order to feel independent, and the Muddler
continued living in his coffee tin.

I took over the pilot-house with a certain melancholy feeling. It was set up on a lonely rock by the
shore, where it most of all resembled a piece of
wreckage. I remember so very clearly looking at
Hodgkins's old tool-chest, which the Hemulens of
the Autocratic Guard had discarded because it
wasn't fine enough for a royal inventor.

I thought, "Now is the time I ought to think up

something that's as remarkable as his inventions. How will I be able to impress my colony? They're all waiting for it, and very soon it will be Friday, and I've been talking much too much about how talented I am . . ."

For a moment I felt quite sick. I looked at the waves rolling past, and I had a vision of Hodgkins just constructing and constructing and constructing and making new inventions all the time, and totally forgetting me.

I very nearly wished that I had been born a Hattifattener under the Hattifatteners' vague and drifting stars, and that no one expected anything else of me than that I also should be drifting along towards an unattainable horizon, never speaking to anyone and never mindful of anything.

This sad state of mind lasted until dusk. Then I began to long for company and went strolling inland from the shore, over the hills where the Autocrat's subjects were building their aimless stone walls, as usual, and having their picnics. They had lighted little camp-fires everywhere, and now and then they fired home-made rockets or cheered their King. I passed the Muddler's tin and heard him conducting an endless monologue. As far as I could comprehend, it was about the shape of a certain button that was round but seen from another angle could also be called oval . . . The Joxter was asleep in his tree, and the Mymble's daughter was probably running about somewhere in order to show her mother that she was independent.

With a deep feeling of the uselessness of everything, I walked to the Garden of Surprises, where all was silent. The waterfalls were shut off and the lanterns dark. The merry-go-round was asleep under a wide brownish cover. The Autocrat's throne was covered also, and under it stood his fog-horn. The ground was strewn with toffee papers.

Then I heard the sound of hammering.

"Hodgkins!" I cried. But he just went on hammering. I blew the fog-horn. After a while I saw Hodgkins's ears penetrate the dusk. He said, "You shouldn't look before it's finished. You're too early."

"I'm not going to look at your invention," I replied sadly. "I want to talk!"

"What about?" he asked.

I was silent for a bit. Then I said, "Hodgkins, please, what does an outlaw and adventurer *do*?"

"Whatever he likes," Hodgkins replied. "Anything else you wanted to know? I'm a little busy." He wiggled his ears in a friendly way and disappeared in the dusk. After a while I heard him hammering again. I walked back home. My head was awhirl with thoughts I really had no need of, and for the first time I found no pleasure at all in thinking about myself. I had sunk into a state of deep gloom, which has also come over me at times later in my life when other people are achieving more than I myself.

But in a way I found this new feeling quite interesting, and I suspected that in spite of everything, it had something to do with being talented. I noticed that if I allowed myself to feel really lugubrious, sighing and staring out over the sea, I began to feel almost contented. I felt such a *colossal* pity for myself. A fascinating experience.

While this was going on, I distractedly started to make some small changes in the pilot-house, using Hodgkins's tools and some pieces of flotsam and wreckage from the shore. I had an idea that the house wasn't tall enough.

This sad, and to my development so important, week passed slowly. I hammered and brooded, and sawed and brooded, and didn't feel a single "click" of the sort I'd felt before.

Thursday night, the moon was full. It was a totally silent night. Even the Autocrat's subjects had tired of cheering and setting off fireworks. I had finished the stairs up to the second storey and was sitting by the window with my nose in my paws, and the night was so silent that you could hear the sphinx-moths brushing their wings.

I caught sight of a small white shape down on the sandy beach. At first it looked like a Hattifattener. But when it came nearer with curious gliding movements, I saw something to raise my bristles. The Being was transparent. I could see the stones and rocks quite clearly through it, and it cast no shadow! If I add that it was draped in something that looked like a thin white sheet, it should be clear to everyone that this was a ghost!

I rose excitedly. Did I close the door downstairs? Perhaps ghosts pass through closed doors . . . ? What should I do? Now the outer door squeaked. A cold draught came flying up the stairs and blew against my neck.

Now, afterwards, I doubt that I was really frightened. I probably only thought that I had every reason to be careful. Because of this I crawled resolutely under the bed and waited. After a little while there was a creak on the stairs. One small creak, and then one more. There were nine steps, I knew very well, because they had been difficult to construct (it was a spiral staircase). So I could count nine creakings, and then all was completely silent, and I thought, "Now it's standing behind the door . . ."

Here Moominpappa stopped reading and made a pause for effect.

"Sniff," he said, "turn up the oil lamp a bit, will you. Just think, my paws get all moist when I read about that ghostly night!"

"Did anybody say something?" mumbled Sniff, waking up.

Moominpappa looked at Sniff and said, "By all means. It was only I, reading from my Memoirs."

"The ghost is fine," said Moomintroll, who was lying with his eider-down up to his ears. "You should keep it. But all those sad feelings, I think, are a bit unnecessary. It's all so long."

"Long?" cried Moominpappa, hurt. "What do you mean, long? Memoirs should have some sad parts. All Memoirs have them. I was having a crisis."

"A what?" asked Sniff.

"I felt ghastly," explained Moominpappa crossly. "Terrible. I was so unhappy that I hardly noticed that I had built myself a two-storey house!"

"Were there apples on the Joxter's apple tree?" asked Snufkin.

"No," replied Moominpappa curtly. He rose and closed his exercise book.

"Daddy, this ghost was really good," said Moomintroll. "Yes. We all think that the ghost is thrilling."

But Moominpappa went down and seated himself in the drawing-room and looked at the aneroid barometer, which he kept hanging over the chest of drawers. Yet this was no pilot-house; this was a drawing-room. What had Hodgkins said when he saw Moominpappa's house? *"You've really been exerting yourself, I can see!"*—in a patronizing way. The others hadn't even noticed that the house had been rebuilt and was higher. Perhaps he ought to shorten that chapter about feelings. Perhaps it seemed silly and not moving at all. Perhaps the whole book was silly.

"Are you sitting here in the dark?" said Moominmamma, by the kitchen door. She had been to the scullery and made a couple of sandwiches.

"I believe the chapter about the crisis of my youth is silly," said Moominpappa.

"Do you mean the beginning of the sixth?" she asked.

Moominpappa mumbled something.

"It's among the best things in the book," said

Moominmamma. "Everything'll be much more vivid
if you have some passages where you aren't bragging.
The children are too small to understand that. I've
made a night sandwich for you, too, for supper. Good
night!"

She went upstairs. The stairs creaked in the same
way as in the old house. Nine creaks. But this
staircase was very much better made than the old
one . . .

Moominpappa ate his sandwich, sitting in the
dark. Then he, too, went upstairs to continue reading
to Moomintroll, Snufkin, and Sniff.

The door opened slightly and very slowly, and a
little white wisp of smoke floated through the crack
and curled up on the carpet. Two pale and shining
eyes blinked at the top of this curl. I saw it all very
clearly from my hiding place under the bed.

"It really is a ghost," I said to myself (it was
absolutely much less frightening to look at it than to
listen to it coming up the stairs). The room had
grown just as cold as rooms tend to grow in ghost
stories; there was a draught from all directions, and
suddenly the ghost sneezed.

Dear reader, I can't know how you would have
felt, but as for me, I lost much of my respect for that
ghost. I crawled out from under the bed (it had seen
me already anyway) and said, "Bless you!"

"And bless *you!*" replied the ghost vexedly. "This
bleak night of fate resounds with the wails of the
phantoms of the gorge!"

"Can I help you with anything?" I asked.

"On a night of fate like this," the ghost resumed stubbornly, "the forgotten bones are rattling on the silent beach!"

"Whose bones?" I wondered.

"The *forgotten* bones," said the ghost. "Pale horror grins over the damnèd island. Mortal, beware: I shall return at midnight on Friday the thirteenth instant!" And the ghost uncurled, gave me a terrible look, and floated back towards the half-open door. The next moment the back of its head met the door-jamb with a resounding bang, and with a cry of "Ow—oops!" it went streaming down the stairs and out into the moonlight, where it howled three times like a hyena. Only by then it was a little late to make an impression.

I saw the ghost dissolve into a wisp of mist and sail off over the sea, and suddenly I laughed. Now I had a surprise for my colony! Now I could do a gruesome deed that nobody else dared to do!

A little before midnight on Friday the thirteenth, I received my colonists on the beach below the pilot-house. The evening was beautifully mild. I was serving a simple meal on the sand: soup, ship's biscuits, and the Autocrat's apple wine (free for anyone to draw from great vats at every crossroads). I had painted the dishes with black bicycle lacquer and decorated them with cross-bones in white.

"I could have given you some red paint," said the Muddler. "Or yellow, or blue. Excuse me, but wouldn't that have been cosier?"

"I don't intend to make it cosy," I replied with some reserve. "Unmentionably terrible things are going to happen tonight. Be prepared."

"This tastes a little like fish soup. Cod, is it?" asked the Joxter.

"Carrots," I replied curtly. "Just keep eating. You probably think that ghosts are common as dust!"

"Oh, I see. You're going to tell ghost stories," said the Joxter.

"I like ghost stories," exclaimed the Mymble's daughter. "Mother always tries to scare us with horror stories at bedtime. She goes on and on, and finally she's so scared herself that we have to keep awake half the night until she's calmed down. My uncle is worse still. Once he—"

"I'm serious," I interrupted her angrily. "Ghost stories—my tail! I'll *give* you a ghost! A real one! I'll invent it, I'll call it! Now what do you say?"

I gave them a triumphant look.

The Mymble's daughter began clapping her paws, but the Muddler looked a bit teary-eyed and whispered, "Please don't! No, no, please don't!"

"For your sake I'll call forth quite a small one," I said protectively.

The Joxter stopped eating and looked at me with surprise—well, even admiration! I had reached my goal and saved my honour! But, dear reader, you may imagine the worry that filled me before it finally became midnight. Would the ghost return? Would it be fearful enough? Would it sneeze and talk balderdash and spoil the effect it should make?

One of my characteristics is wanting to make an

impression at any price by awakening admiration, sympathy, fright, or, on the whole, *any* feelings that include interest. That's probably because of my unappreciated childhood.

Anyway, as the clock neared the hour of twelve, I clambered up on a rock, lifted my nose to the moon, waved my paws magically about, and uttered a sort of ululation intended to pierce bone and marrow. In other words, I called forth the ghost.

The colonists sat bewitched from excitement and expectation. Only in the Joxter's water-clear critical eyes could I glimpse a hint of disbelief. To this day I feel a deep contentment that even the Joxter was impressed. Because the ghost did arrive. It really arrived—luminous, transparent, and shadowless—and immediately started talking about the forgotten bones and the phantoms of the gorge.

The Muddler gave a shriek and hid his head in the sand, but the Mymble's daughter walked straight up to the ghost, held out her paw, and said, "Hello! What fun to meet a real ghost. Would you like some soup?"

You never know what Mymbles may be up to.

Of course, my ghost felt insulted. It found itself at a loss; it shrank a bit and crumpled. Just as the poor ghost disappeared in a sad wisp of smoke the Joxter started to laugh, and I'm sure the ghost heard it. Well, the night was spoiled.

But the colonists were to pay dearly for their inexcusable tactlessness. The following week was indescribable. None of us could sleep at night. The ghost brought an iron chain and rattled it until four o'clock in the morning, in addition to all the owl hoots and hyena howls and shuffling steps and knockings and furniture jumping about and breaking.

The colonists complained.

"Take away your ghost," said the Joxter. "We want to sleep!"

"That isn't possible," I explained gravely. "Once you have called forth a ghost you have to keep it."

"The Muddler's crying," said the Joxter reproachfully. "The ghost has painted a skull on his tin and written POISON under it, and now the Muddler is beside himself and says it's a warning that means he'll never marry!"

"How childish," I said.

"Yes, but Hodgkins is angry!" the Joxter continued. "Your ghost has painted warnings all over the *Oshun Oxtra* and has been pinching his wire springs!"

"In that case," I exclaimed agitatedly, "we'll have to do something about it! At once!"

I hastily composed a message and nailed it to the door of the pilot-house. It went as follows:

> *Dear Ghost!*
> *For obvious reasons a Ghost Council will be held next Friday before sunset. All complaints will be attended to.*
> BOARD OF THE
ROYAL OUTLAW COLONY
> *P.S. No chains to be brought.*

I thought long about whether to write Royal or Outlaw. Finally I decided on both. They balanced nicely.

The ghost replied with red paint on parchment (the parchment was found to be Hodgkins's old raincoat, pinned to the door with the Mymble's breadknife):

> *The Hour of Fate is nearing. Friday,* but *at Midnight, when the Hound of Death is howling in the lonely wilderness! Vain creatures, hide your snouts in the cold earth that rings with the heavy tread of the Invisible, because your Fate is written in blood on the wall of the Tomb! I'll bring my chain if I like.*
> THE GHOST,
CALLED THE HORRIBLEST

"Well," said the Joxter. "Fate's a word he's fond of."

"Mind that you don't laugh this time," I said severely. "This is what comes of having no respect for anything in life!"

The Muddler was sent to invite Hodgkins to the Ghost Council. I could have gone myself, of course, but I remembered what Hodgkins had said to me: "You shouldn't look before it's finished. You're too early. I'm a little busy." Just like that, in quite a friendly but very distant voice.

The ghost arrived at twelve o'clock sharp and greeted us with three hollow howls. "I have come!" it said in its inimitable tones. "Tremble, mortals, for the revenge of the forgotten bones!"

"Evening," said the Joxter. "What are these old bones you're always going on about? Whose are they? Can't you find them yourself?"

I kicked the Joxter on the shins and said politely, "We greet you, Phantom of the Gorge! How are you? Pale horror grins over this damnèd coast."

"Leave my lines alone!" said the ghost angrily. "That's the way I'm supposed to speak!"

"Now, listen," said Hodgkins. "Can't you let us sleep in peace? Can't you go and frighten someone else?"

"Everybody's accustomed to me," said the ghost gruffly. "Not even Edward the Booble is frightened any more."

"I was!" cried the Muddler. "I'm frightened still!"

"That's nice of you," said the ghost and added

hastily, "The lost skeleton caravan is howling under the ice-green moon!"

"Dear ghost," said Hodgkins kindly, "you seem to have lost your poise somewhat. Listen. *You* promise to frighten people somewhere else, and *I* promise to teach you new ways of doing it. All right?"

"Hodgkins is good at grisly things!" cried the Mymble's daughter. "You've no idea of what he can make from a spot of phosphorus and some sheet metal! You could frighten Edward the Booble silly!"

"And the Autocrat," I added.

The ghost gave Hodgkins a hesitant look.

"A fog-horn of your own?" Hodgkins suggested. "Do you know the thread-and-resin trick?"

"No. Tell me!" said the ghost with interest.

"Sewing thread, thick sort," explained Hodgkins. "Number twenty or less. You attach it to somebody's window. You stand outside and rub the thread with resin. Horrible noises."

"By my demon eye, you're a real friend," cried the ghost and curled up at Hodgkins's feet. "Could you get me a skeleton of my own? Who said sheet metal? I have some of that. How should I use it?"

Then Hodgkins sat half the night describing devices for scaring people, and drawing the constructions in the sand. He seemed clearly engrossed by this childish occupation.

In the morning he went back to the Garden of Surprises, and my ghost was elected a member of the Royal Outlaw Colony with the honorary title of the Terror of Horror Island.

"Listen, ghost," I said, "would you like to live with me? I'm feeling a bit lonesome. Now, of course I'm not the sort to be afraid, but some nights *are* a bit boring . . ."

"By all the Hounds of Hell," began the ghost, paling even more with annoyance. But it calmed down presently and replied, "Well, why not? That's very kind of you."

I made him a bed out of a packing-case that I painted black with a decoration of cross-bones (to make him feel at home). The feeding bowl I marked POISON (to the Muddler's great satisfaction).

"Most cosy," said the ghost. "Please don't mind if I rattle a bit at midnight. It's a habit."

"Rattle all you want to," I said. "But not more than five minutes, and please keep away from the meerschaum tram. It's very valuable."

"Well, five minutes, then," said the ghost. "But I won't make any promises about Midsummer Night."

CHAPTER VII

In which I describe the triumphant unveiling of the converted Oshun Oxtra *and an eventful trial dive to the bottom of the sea.*

n Midsummer Eve, the Mymble gave birth to her smallest daughter and named her My, which means the-smallest-in-existence. And Midsummer Night came and went, and the trees blossomed, and the blossoms changed into apples or other good things and were eaten, and somehow or other I slipped into a perilous routine that took me so far that I even planted velvet roses on the bridge of the pilot-house and started playing tiddly-winks with the Muddler and the Autocrat.

Nothing was happening. My little ghost sat in the corner by the stove knitting scarves and socks, a very calming occupation for weak-nerved ghosts. At first it had really succeeded in frightening the Autocrat's subjects and had been very happy, but it stopped ghosting when it noticed that the subjects liked their frights.

The Mymble's daughter fibbed more than ever and fooled me every time. Once she spread the rumour that Edward the Booble had happened to trample the Autocrat to bits! I'm afraid I always believe what people are telling me, and I'm quite hurt when I find that they've been fibbing or having fun at my expense. When I exaggerate, I even believe myself!

Sometimes Edward the Booble came along and stood in the shallow water by the beach and bawled us out by force of habit. Then the Joxter bawled back at him; otherwise I never saw him do anything except eat, sleep, sun himself, laugh with the Mymble, and climb trees. At first he also used to climb over stone walls, but soon tired of it when he discovered that it wasn't forbidden. But he said he had a good time.

Occasionally I could see the Hattifatteners sailing along far out to sea, and that made me melancholy for the rest of the day.

During this time I developed that restlessness which now sometimes makes me quite tired of a well-ordered and uneventful life and suddenly wanting to take off, so to speak.

But then, finally, it happened.

One day Hodgkins himself was standing by the door of the pilot-house, and he had donned his captain's cap. Only now it was adorned with a pair of small golden wings!

I ran down the stairs and shouted, "Hodgkins! Hello! You've made it fly!"

He waggled his ears and nodded.

"Have you told anybody?" I asked with a beating heart.

He shook his head. And immediately I was an adventurer once again, my zest returned, I felt big and strong and handsome! Hodgkins had come to tell *me* first of all that his invention was finished! Not even the Autocrat knew it.

"Quick! Quick!" I cried. "Let's pack! I'll give my velvet roses away! I'll give my house away! Oh, Hodgkins, I'm bursting with ideas and expectations!"

"That's good," said Hodgkins. "But first there's the unveiling and trial flight. We can't cheat the Autocrat out of a party."

The trial flight took place that same afternoon. The transformed river-boat was standing on a platform before the Autocrat's throne, shrouded in a red cloth.

"A black one would have been more festive," observed my ghost, clattering its knitting-needles. "Or a veil, ashen pale as midnight fog. The shade of horror, you know."

"What a prattler he is," said the Mymble, who had brought all her children to the event. "Hello, dearest daughter! Come and look at your latest brothers and sisters!"

"Mother dear," said the Mymble's daughter, "have you made new ones again? Tell them that their sister is a Royal Colonial Princess on her way to a trip around the moon in a flying river-boat!"

The Mymble children bobbed, nodded, and stared.

Hodgkins disappeared several times behind the canvas drapery to inspect something or other. "Something's the matter with the exhaust pipe," he mumbled. "Joxter! Go aboard, will you, and switch on the big fan!"

After a while the big fan was heard to start. Almost at once a large lump of oatmeal porridge came flying out from the exhaust pipe and hit Hodgkins in the eye.

"There's something wrong," he said. "Oatmeal porridge!"

The Mymbles shouted ecstatically.

"Excuse me," cried the Muddler, near to tears. "I put the left-overs from breakfast into the teapot, *not* in the exhaust!"

"What's up?" asked the Autocrat. "May We begin Our speech, or are you too busy?"

"That was just my little daughter My," explained the Mymble delightedly. "Such a little personality already! Porridge in an exhaust pipe! What inventiveness!"

"Don't take it too seriously, madam," said Hodgkins, a bit stiffly.

"May We begin or may We not?" asked the King.

"Please, Your Majesty, go ahead," I said.

After a pause for the fog-horn, the Hemulic Voluntary Brass Band stood at attention, and the Autocrat climbed to his throne amid general cheering. When all was silent again he spoke: "Dear foggy-headed subjects! The occasion calls for a few solemn words. Take a good look at Hodgkins, Our Royal Inventor of Surprises! His greatest one is to be unveiled today to start on its pioneer voyage over land, through water and air. Please keep this bold enterprise somewhere at the back of your fuzzy minds when you are sniffing around in your cosy corners, gnawing, poking about, and talking nonsense. We are still expecting great things of you, dearest disastrous, unsatisfactory subjects. Try to spread a little honour over Our hills, and if you can't do that, then at least give the hero of the day your best cheers!"

And the people cheered enthusiastically.

The Hemulens struck up the Royal Festiwaltz, and amidst a shower of roses and artificial pearls, Hodgkins went up to the platform and pulled the silk rope. What a moment!

The drape slid to the ground.

But this was no longer our old river-boat; it was a winged metal thing, a strange machine! It made me quite melancholy. Then I noticed something to reconcile me to the transformation of the ship—its name was painted in ultramarine, and it was the *Oshun Oxtra* as before!

The Hemulic band changed over to the Autocratical Anthem (you know, with the refrain "Surprised, aren't you? Ha-ha!"), and the Mymble, always easily moved, wept happy tears.

Hodgkins tugged at the peak of his cap and went aboard, followed by the Royal Outlaw Colony (with roses and artificial pearls still raining over us), and the *Oshun Oxtra* was overrun by Mymble children.

"Excuse me!" the Muddler suddenly cried, and jumped back over the gangway. "By my buttons, I daren't! Not in the air! I'll be sick again!" He rushed off and disappeared into the crowd.

Just then the machine began to vibrate and hum. All the doors were closed and bolted, and the *Oshun Oxtra* swayed hesitantly back and forth on its platform. At the next moment it took such a sudden leap that I tumbled off my feet.

When I dared to look out of a window, we were cruising along over the tree-tops of the Garden of Surprises.

"It's flying! It's flying!" cried the Joxter.

I cannot find words to describe the singular feeling that filled me as I hovered over the earth. Even if I'm quite satisfied with the outline, so to speak, that has been given me by an inscrutable fate, I must admit that it is not intended for hovering in the air. Now, suddenly, I felt light and elegant like a swallow, I had no care in the world, I was fast as lightning and invincible. Most of all, I was exquisitely amused by all those people toddling along down on the ground or staring up at me in awed admiration. It was a wonderful moment, only too brief.

The *Oshun Oxtra* was swooping softly downwards and was soon ploughing along, with white moustaches of foam, through the sea by the Autocrat's coast.

"Hodgkins!" I cried. "Let's fly again!"

He looked at me without seeing me, his eyes shone very blue, his whole person bore the marks of a secret triumph that had nothing to do with us around him. And then he steered the *Oshun Oxtra* straight down into the water. The cabin was filled by a green, transparent light, and swarms of bubbles went dancing across the portholes.

"We'll never come up," said Little My.

I pressed my nose to the glass and looked out into the sea. The *Oshun Oxtra* had lighted a ring of lanterns amidships. They sent a weak, trembling glow into the deep-sea dark.

I shuddered. Nothing but green darkness in all directions. We were hovering in an eternal night, in complete emptiness. Hodgkins cut off the engine, and we sank and glided deeper and deeper down. No one said a word. We were all a bit scared, as a matter of fact.

But Hodgkins's ears were pointing straight out with joy and happiness, and now I saw that he had donned a new captain's cap, decorated with two small fins of silver.

In that tremendous silence I began to hear a stifled murmuring that grew louder and louder. It sounded like thousands of scared voices whispering the same word over and over, one single word: "Sea-Hound, Sea-Hound, Sea-Hound . . ."

Dear reader, try to whisper "Sea-Hound" a couple of times, warningly and very slowly—it sounds gruesome!

Now we could discern a lot of small shadowy shapes nearing in the darkness. They were fishes and sea-serpents, and every one of them carried a small lantern on its nose.

"Why haven't they lighted their lanterns?" wondered the Mymble.

"Perhaps their batteries are flat," her daughter said. "Who's the Sea-Hound, Mother?"

The fishes swam right up to the *Oshun Oxtra* and seemed most interested. They remained in a dense circle around the diving ship, and all along we could hear their frightened whispering: "Sea-Hound! Sea-Hound!"

"This can't be right," said the Joxter. "I have Forebodings! I can feel it in my nose that they don't

dare light their lanterns. Just think that somebody's *forbidding* them to light the lanterns they're carrying on their own heads!"

"The Sea-Hound, perhaps?" whispered the Mymble's daughter, glowing with excitement. "I had an aunt who never dared to light her spirit stove, because the first time she did it, everything blew up, and her with it!"

"We'll all burn," said Little My.

The fishes squeezed nearer. They now formed a continuous wall around the *Oshun Oxtra*, looking in at our lights.

"Are they saying anything else?" I asked.

At that Hodgkins switched on his wireless listening apparatus. There was a buzzing, and then we could hear a thousandfold worried shouts: "Sea-Hound! Sea-Hound! He's approaching, he's much nearer now . . . Put out the lights! Put out the lights! He'll eat you . . . How many watts do you carry, poor whale?"

"Darkness should be really dark," said my ghost understandingly. "The night of fate veils the cemetery in black shrouds; black wraiths are flitting through the dark with dejected wails."

"Hush hush hush," said Hodgkins. "I hear something else . . ."

We listened. Far away there was a faint throb, like a pulse—no, like steps, as if something were bounding nearer in great, slow leaps. In a moment all the fishes disappeared.

"We'll all be eaten now," said Little My.

"I believe I'll put the children to bed," said the Mymble. "Now, to bed, all of you!"

Her children stood themselves in a circle and helped each other with the buttons on their backs.

"Count yourselves tonight," said the Mymble. "I feel a little distracted."

"Aren't you going to read to us?" the children cried.

"Well, yes, why not," said the Mymble. "Where did we stop last time?"

The children chorused, " 'This - is - One - eyed - Bob's - sanguinary - work' - remarked - Inspector - Twiggs - pulling - a - three - inch - nail - from - the - ear - of - the - corpse - 'it - must - have - happened'—"

"Quite, quite," said the Mymble. "But hurry up a bit, please . . ."

The strange bouncing sound was much nearer now. The *Oshun Oxtra* was rocking agitatedly, and the listening apparatus hissed like a cat. I felt my neck bristles rise, and cried, "Hodgkins! Put out the lights!"

Before darkness fell, we caught sight of the Sea-Hound to starboard, and this glimpse was indescribably eerie—perhaps particularly because we only got a kind of general impression of the beast. In the darkness I imagined the rest, and that was worse still.

Hodgkins started the engine, but he probably was too upset to be able to navigate. Instead of rising to the surface, the *Oshun Oxtra* speedily dived down to the bottom of the sea.

There she started up her caterpillar tracks and began crawling over the sand. Algae glided across our portholes like groping hands. In the darkness and silence we could hear the panting of the Sea-Hound. Now he appeared among the seaweed like a grey shadow. His eyes were yellow and shone like a couple of searchlights moving over the sides of the ship.

"Under the covers, children!" the Mymble shouted. "And don't come out until I tell you to!"

There was a sickening wrench and a crash astern. The Sea-Hound had started on the rudder.

Suddenly there followed a great upheaval in the sea. The *Oshun Oxtra* rose tail-upwards and was thrown over on its back, seaweed streamed and slithered along the sea-bed like wind-blown hair, and the water roared like a bath tap. We were thrown head over heels, all the cupboards flew open, the crockery

came crashing out and was rolling about on the floor with oatmeal, sago, rice, and tea, the Mymble children's boots and the ghost's knitting-needles, and the Joxter's tobacco from his tin. And from outside came a roar that made the bristles rise on every tail.

Then all became silent. Eerily silent.

"I like flying very much," declared the Mymble candidly, "but diving not at all. I wonder how many children I have left. Count them, dearest daughter!"

But the Mymble's daughter had but begun her task when we heard a terrible voice that shouted, "Ah-ha! Here you are, you grokely dishrags! By all my seven hundred scales of my scaly tail! Did you think you could hide down there, what? Not a chance! Always forgetting to tell me where you're going, what?"

"Who's that, now?" cried the Mymble.

"I'll give you three guesses," said the Joxter and grinned.

Hodgkins turned on the lamps, and Edward the Booble thrust his head under water and looked in at us through a porthole. We looked back at him as composedly as possible, and then we noticed a few small pieces of Sea-Hound floating about: a bit of tail and a bit of whisker and some flat pieces, but mainly a sort of mash, because Edward the Booble had happened to tread on him.

"Edward! My true friend!" Hodgkins cried.

"We'll never forget this," said I. "You saved us at the last moment!"

"Give the kind gentleman a kiss, children," cried the Mymble, and started to cry from emotion.

"What's that?" said Edward the Booble. "Don't let out any kiddies, please. They always get in my ears. You're worse and worse every day! Soon you'll be quite uneatable. I've stubbed my toes looking for you everywhere, and now you're trying to wheedle yourself out of this as usual."

"You've trodden the Sea-Hound to a pulp!" cried the Joxter.

"Eh?" said the Booble and jumped back. "Somebody again? Believe me, it wasn't my fault! And I really *haven't* the money for any more funerals . . ." Suddenly he got quite angry and shouted, "Anyway, why don't you keep your old dogs out of harm's way! Blame yourself!"

And Edward the Booble went wading away. He looked deeply hurt. After a while he turned round and bellowed, "I'm coming for tea in the morning! And make it strong!"

Suddenly something happened again—all the sea bottom was lit up.

"We'll burn up again," said Little My.

A million billion fishes came swimming from everywhere with blazing lanterns, pocket lights, searchlights, bull's-eyes, bulbs, and acetylene lamps. Some of them carried a bracket lamp at each ear, and they were all beside themselves with joy and gratitude.

The sea, a while ago so bleak, became illuminated in rainbow colours by violet, red, and chrome-yellow sea-anemones on a blue lawn, and the sea-serpents wheeled and turned somersaults from happiness.

We sailed home in triumph, criss-crossing over the ocean, and we never quite knew whether the lights that shone in through our portholes were stars or fishes.

Towards morning we steered back to the Autocrat's island, and by then most of us felt rather limp and sleepy.

Little My
magnified greatly

CHAPTER VIII

In which I give an account of the circumstances of the Muddler's wedding, further touch slightly on my dramatic meeting with Moominmamma, and finally write the profound closing words of my Memoirs.

Ten miles (nautical) off the coast, we sighted a dinghy carrying a signal of distress.

"It's the Autocrat," I cried in shocked tones. "Do you think there can have been a revolution so early in the morning?" (Only perhaps the King's subjects weren't of that disposition.)

"Revolution?" Hodgkins said and changed to full speed ahead. "I hope my nephew's safe."

"What's up?" the Mymble shouted when we stopped by the Royal dinghy.

"Up? Up!" cried the Autocrat. "Everything's up —I mean down. You'll have to come home at once."

"Have the forgotten bones extracted their revenge at last?" asked the ghost hopefully.

"It's your little Muddler who is responsible for it all," panted the Autocrat as he climbed aboard. "(Take care of the dinghy, somebody!) We came out to meet you Ourselves because We don't trust any of Our subjects."

"The Muddler!" exclaimed the Joxter.

"Exactly," replied the King. "We like weddings very much, but We simply *can't* let seven thousand Niblings and a savage Aunt into Our kingdom."

"Who's marrying?" asked the Mymble interestedly.

"I said it, didn't I? The Muddler!" replied the Autocrat.

"Impossible," said Hodgkins.

"Impossible or not, the wedding's today!" said the Autocrat nervously. "With a Fuzzy. (Full speed ahead, please!) Well, they fell head over heels in love at first sight, and they've been swapping buttons and running about being generally silly ever since, and now they've sent a telegram to an Aunt—but the Muddler says she's possibly been eaten—and to seven thousand Niblings and invited them all to the wedding! And We're willing to eat Our crown that they'll be gnawing Our realm to bits! Give Us a glass of wine, somebody, please!"

"Could it be that they've invited the *Hemulen Aunt*?" I asked, greatly shocked, and handed the Autocrat his drink.

"Yes, yes, something like that," he replied dejectedly. "An Aunt with only half a snout, and ill-tempered into the bargain. We are all for surprises, but We like to make them Ourselves."

We were nearing the coast.

Out on the point, the Muddler stood waiting with the Fuzzy at his side. The *Oshun Oxtra* put in at the landing-stage, and Hodgkins threw the hawser to a couple of subjects that were admiring us. "We-ell?" he said.

"Excuse me!" the Muddler cried. "I'm married!"

"Me too!" the Fuzzy said, and dropped a curtsy.

"But We told you to wait until the afternoon, didn't We?" lamented the Autocrat. "Now we won't have the same fun at the wedding party!"

"Excuse me, please, we couldn't wait," said the Muddler. "We're so much in love!"

"Oh, dear me, dear me!" cried the Mymble and rushed sobbing down the gangway. "The best of luck to you both! What a sweet little Fuzzy! Give them three cheers, children, they're married!"

"They're past helping now," said Little My.

At this point, Moominpappa was cut short by Sniff, who sat up in his bed and cried, "Stop!"

"Father's reading about his youth," said Moomintroll reproachfully.

"And about my *daddy's youth," replied Sniff with unexpected dignity. "I've heard a lot about the Muddler so far, but never a word about any Fuzzy!"*

"I forgot about her," mumbled Moominpappa. "She came into the story only now . . ."

"You forgot my mother!" *Sniff cried.*

The door to the bedroom opened and Moominmamma looked in. "Still awake?" she said. "Did I hear somebody cry for Mother?"

"It was me," Sniff said and jumped out of his bed. "Just think of it! Here we've heard lots and lots about daddies, and then suddenly without warning one learns that there's a mother as well!"

"But that's natural, isn't it?" replied Moominmamma with some surprise. "As far as I know, your mother turned out very well and had a large button collection."

Sniff gave Moominpappa a stern look and said, "Well?"

"Several collections!" Moominpappa assured him. "Stones, shells, glass beads, you name it! And anyway, she was *a surprise!"*

Sniff sank into thoughts.

"Speaking of mothers," said Snufkin. "This Mymble, as a matter of fact. Did I have a mother, too?"

"Of course!" said Moominpappa. "And a very nice round one indeed."

"Then Little My's a relation?" Snufkin cried wonderingly.

"Certainly, certainly!" said Moominpappa. "But please don't interrupt me, now. These are really my Memoirs, and not a genealogical table!"

"May he read?" asked Moomintroll.

"Well . . ." Sniff and Snufkin consented.

"Thanks!" said Moominpappa, relieved, and continued his reading.

The Muddler and the Fuzzy received wedding presents all through the day. Finally the coffee tin was filled to the brim, and the rest of the buttons, stones, shells, doorknobs, and other things (too many to be listed here) had to be heaped on the rocks beside it.

The Muddler sat down on the heap and held the Fuzzy's paw and was beside himself with joy.

"It's grand to be married," he said.

"Possibly," Hodgkins remarked. "But listen, please. Did you *have* to invite the Hemulen Aunt? And the Niblings?"

"Excuse me, but I was afraid to hurt their feelings," the Muddler said.

"Yes, but the Aunt—the Aunt!" I cried.

"Well," answered the Muddler, "to be frank, I haven't missed her terribly. But excuse me! I've such a guilty conscience! Remember I wished for some-body to be so kind as to eat her?"

"Mphm," Hodgkins said. "Well, you have a point there."

On the following day, when the packet-boat was due to arrive, the landing-stage, the hills, and the beaches were thronged with the Autocrat's subjects. His Majesty's canopied throne was set up on the highest hill, and he was all ready to give his starting signal to the Hemulic Voluntary Brass Band.

The Muddler and the Fuzzy were seated in a special wedding boat, in the shape of a swan.

Everybody was feeling excited and a little uneasy, because the rumours of the Hemulen Aunt and her character had spread all over the kingdom. More-over, people had every reason to be afraid that the Niblings would undermine the country and gnaw the trees in the Garden of Surprises to pieces. But nobody said a word about this to the newly wedded couple, who sat peacefully swapping buttons.

"Do you think she could be scared off with phos-phorus or with thread-and-resin?" asked my ghost, who sat embroidering skulls on a tea-cosy for the Fuzzy.

"Not she," I replied.

"She'll be starting educational games again," the Joxter prophesied. "Perhaps she'll even keep us from hibernating when winter comes, and make us *ski!*"

"What's that?" the Mymble's daughter asked.

"Slithering on atmospheric precipitation," Hodg-kins explained.

"Dear me!" cried the Mymble. "How fearful!"

"We'll die of it," said Little My.

Now a frightened murmur rippled through the waiting crowd. The packet-boat was nearing.

The Hemulic Band launched into the anthem "Save Our Silly People," and the wedding swan put out to sea. Two Mymble children fell into the water from pure excitement, the fog-horns blared, and the Joxter lost his nerve and fled.

Only after we noticed that the packet-boat was empty did it dawn upon us that it couldn't ever have held as many as seven thousand Niblings. Cries of relief, mixed with disappointment, were heard along the beach. One single little Nibling jumped down into the wedding swan, which now turned back towards the quay at good speed.

"What's this?" said the Autocrat, who hadn't been able to hold himself back and had left his throne and walked down to the beach. *"One single Nibling?"*

"It's our own old Nibling!" I cried. "And he's carrying a colossal parcel!"

"So she was eaten after all," Hodgkins said.

"Silence! Silence! Silence!" shouted the King and started his fog-horn. "Make way for the Nibling! He's an Ambassador!"

The crowd made room for the bridal couple and the Nibling, who shyly waddled up to us and laid his parcel on the ground. The edges and corners of it were slightly gnawed, but in general its condition was good.

"Well?" said the Autocrat.

"The Hemulen Aunt sends you her compliments . . ." said the Nibling, wildly searching the pockets of his Sunday coat.

Everybody was jumping with impatience.

"Hurry up, hurry up!" cried the King.

Finally the Nibling found a crumpled letter and explained with dignity, "The Hemulen Aunt has taught me to write. I know nearly all of the alphabet! Every letter except U, V, W, X, Y, and Z! She dictated and I wrote. It goes like this." The Nibling paused for breath and started laboriously to read aloud:

"DEAR CHILDREN!

IT IS ITH THE DEEPEST REGRET, ITH A GILT CONSCIENCE AND A FEELING OF HAING FAILED IN M DT, THAT I RITE O THIS LETTER. I AM REALL NOT ABLE TO COME TO OR EDDING, AND I NDERSTAND THAT I CAN HARDL HOPE FOR OR FORGIENESS. BELIEE ME, I FELT HAPP AND QITE FLATTERED TO HEAR THAT O LONGED TO SEE ME AGAIN, AND I HAE SHED TORRENTS OF HAPP TEARS, I AS SO MOED TO HEAR ABOT THE LITTLE MDDLER'S DECISION TO TAKE ONE OF THE MOST SERIOS STEPS THERE ARE IN LIFE. DEAR CHILDREN, I REALL DO NOT KNO HO TO THANK O: FIRST, THAT O SAED ME FROM THE GROKE, AND SECOND, THAT O ACQAINTED ME ITH THE

DELIGHTFL NIBLINGS. IT IS M DT TO TELL O THE BARE TRTH: THE NIBLINGS AND I HAE SCH FN TOGETHER THAT NOT EEN A EDDING PART CAN DRA S AA FROM HOME. EVER DA E ARE HOLDING QIES AND MLTIPLICATION CONTESTS FOR SE-ERAL HORS AT A STRETCH; AND E ARE LOOKING FORARD EPECTANTL TO THE INTER ITH ITS HEALTH EERCISE IN THE SNO. TO CONSOLE O IN OR DISAPPOINT-MENT, I AM, HOEER, SENDING O A ALA-BLE EDDING PRESENT, AND HOPE IT MA FIND A PERMANENT PLACE IN THE MDDLER'S TIN.

> *ITH 6,999 GREETINGS FROM M FRIENDS!*
> *ORS ER, ER GRATEFLL,*
> *HEMLEN ANT ''*

There was silence on the hills.

"What's 'DT'?" I asked.

"DUTY, of course," replied the Nibling.

"Do you like educational games?" Hodgkins asked cautiously.

"I love them!" said the Nibling.

I sat down and didn't know what to say.

"Won't you be so kind as to open the parcel!" cried the Muddler.

The Nibling solemnly gnawed at the string and produced a full-size photograph of the Hemulen Aunt dressed as Queen of the Niblings.

"Her snout's all there!" the Muddler cried. "I'm so happy! Oh, what a relief!"

"Darling, look at the frame," said the Fuzzy.

We all looked at the frame and cried, "Oh!" It was made of pure Spanish gold set with small roses of topaz and chrysolite in the corners. Small diamonds formed an inner fringe around the portrait. (The back was set with ordinary turquoises.)

"Do you think they can be prised loose?" the Fuzzy asked.

"They certainly can!" cried the Muddler enthusiastically. "Didn't somebody give us an awl?"

And at that moment a terrible voice was heard in the bay and it shouted, "Well! By all that's grokely! I've waited and waited for my morning tea, but not a soul seems to remember old Uncle Edward!"

A couple of days after Moominpappa had read about the Muddler's wedding, he was sitting on the verandah with his family. It was a windy September night. Moominmamma had made them some hot rum punch and treacle sandwiches, and all were dressed in their very best and had decorated themselves in the special way they used only for very solemn events.

"We-ell?" asked Moominmamma expectantly.

"The Memoirs were finished today," Moominpappa announced in a thick voice. "The closing words were put down at six forty-five. And the last sentence—well, you shall decide for yourself!"

"Haven't you written anything about your wicked life with the Hattifatteners?" Snufkin asked.

"No," said Moominpappa. "I want this to be an instructive *book, don't you see."*

"Yes, that's why!" Sniff cried.

"Hush, hush," said Moominmamma. "But won't I come into the picture by and by?" And she blushed quite pink.

Moominpappa took three large swigs from his glass and answered, "Exactly. Listen carefully, my son, because the last part tells of how I found your mother."

Then he opened the book and read:

Autumn came, and great grey rains enveloped the Autocrat's island in a permanent mist.

I had been so certain that our glorious trip in the *Oshun Oxtra* was only an introduction to a great journey out into the world. But this was not the case. It was a culmination, a climax without consequences. As soon as Hodgkins was back home again and the excitement surrounding the Muddler's wedding had lessened, he started to improve his invention. He changed things and added things, he equipped and furnished and trimmed and polished and painted endlessly, and finally the *Oshun Oxtra* looked like a drawing-room inside.

Now and then Hodgkins took the Autocrat or the Royal Outlaw Colony on small pleasure-trips, but he always returned by dinner-time.

I longed to be elsewhere. I shrivelled with my longing for the enormous world that was waiting for me. The rains grew worse and worse, and always

there was something to be adjusted: the diving rudder, or the lighting, or the crankcase lid, or something else that had to be changed.

Then came the great gales.
The Mymble's house blew away, and her daughter got a bad cold from sleeping out-of-doors. The
rain came through into the Muddler's tin. I was the
only one to own a sturdy house with a good stove.
So what does one do? Of course they all lived with
me after a while. And the more there was of family
life in the old pilot-house, the more lonely I felt.

I cannot stress enough the perils of your friends
marrying or becoming court inventors. One day you
are all a society of outlaws, adventurous comrades
and companions who will be pushing off somewhere
or other when things become tiresome; you have
all the world to choose from, just by looking at the
map . . .

. . . And then, suddenly, they're not interested any
more. They want to keep warm. They're afraid of
rain. They start collecting big things that can't fit in
a rucksack. They talk only of small things. They
don't like to make sudden decisions and do something contrariwise. Formerly they hoisted sail; now
they carpenter little shelves for porcelain mugs. Oh,
who can speak of such matters without shedding
tears!

Worst of all, I was infected by it all, and the jollier
I was in their company by the fireside, the harder it
became to feel free and daring like an eagle. Dear
reader, do you understand me? I was shut in, but an

outsider nevertheless, and finally I felt myself to be nothing at all, and there was nothing but gales and rain.

On the special evening I am now going to tell you

about, the weather was terrible indeed. My roof creaked and squeaked, now and then the sou'wester pushed the smoke down the chimney, and the rain was rushing with the sound of little running feet over the verandah (I had rebuilt the captain's bridge into a verandah and had fret-sawed a pine-cone-patterned balustrade).

"Mother! Won't you read to us!" said the Mymble children from their beds.

"Yes," said the Mymble. "Where did we stop?"

"Inspector-Twiggs-silently-crept-to-the-door," the children chorused.

"All right," said their mother. "Inspector Twiggs silently crept to the door. Was that a pistol-barrel that gleamed for a second in the moonlight outside? Coldly determined, he advanced on the feet of Avenging Justice, stopped dead, took a step . . ."

Abstractedly I listened to the Mymble's tale. I had heard it many times.

"I like that story," said the ghost. It was embroidering a sponge-bag (cross-bones on black flannel) while keeping an eye on the clock.

The Muddler and the Fuzzy sat by the fire holding hands. The Joxter played patience. Hodgkins lay on his stomach looking at the pictures in *A Voyage over the Ocean.* All was secure and cosy, family life at its best, and the more I looked at it, the more uneasy did I feel. My legs prickled.

Every now and then a gust of sea-spray washed over the dark and rattling window-panes.

"To be out on a night like this . . ." I mumbled distractedly.

"Eight on the Beaufort scale. Possibly more," concurred Hodgkins, staring at his picture-book waves.

"I'm going to have a look at the weather," I mumbled, and slipped out through the leeward door. For a moment I stood listening on the doorstep.

The dark night was filled with the menacing crash and tumble of the surf. I sniffed at the wind, turned back my ears, and went over to the windward side.

The gale rushed at me with a howl and I closed my eyes to avoid seeing all the unmentionably fiendish things that may be on the move on a stormy autumn night. Gruesome things that are best ignored and shouldn't be thought about . . .

As a matter of fact, this was one of the few times when I didn't think at all. I only knew that I had to go down to the beach and the hissing breakers. It was the kind of magical Foreboding that also later in my life has led to surprising results.

The moon appeared between the night clouds and made the wet sand shine like a metal disc. The waves came thundering in like rows of white dragons, rising high with spread-out claws and crashing down on the beach, creeping back, crackling and hissing, and returning again.

My memories overcome me!

What made me defy the cold and the dark (which all Moomins loathe) to struggle down to the beach on just that purpose-filled night when the sea carried Moomintroll's mother to our island? (O Destiny, exceptional thing!)

Clinging to a spar, she came shooting in with the surf, was carried like a ball into the cove, and was sucked out again with the backwash.

I rushed out in the water and shouted at the top of my voice, "I'm here!"

Now she came back again. She had lost hold of her spar and was floating upside-down with her legs in the air. I did not bat an eyelid before the black wall of seething water. I caught the shipwrecked beauty in my arms. The next second I was swept off my feet, and we were whirling helplessly around in the boiling surf.

With supernatural strength I fought for a foothold —I managed to crawl ashore while the waves hungrily grabbed for my tail, I stumbled, I struggled, I fought—and at last I laid my sweet burden down on the beach, safe from the wild and cruel sea! Oh, this was not in the least like rescuing the Hemulen Aunt! This was a Moomin, like myself, but still more beautiful, a little Moomin woman whom *I* had saved!

She sat up and cried, "Save my handbag! Oh, save my handbag!"

"But you're holding it!" I said.

"Oh, so I am," she exclaimed. "Thank heavens . . ." And she opened her large black handbag and started rummaging in its depths. At last she found her powder compact.

"I'm afraid my powder's sea-damaged," she said sadly.

"You're every bit as beautiful without it," I replied gallantly.

At that she gave me an unfathomable look and blushed deeply.

Let me stop here, at this remarkable turning-point of my stormy youth, let me close my Memoirs at the moment when the most wonderful of Moomins comes into my life! Since then my follies have been supervised by her gentle and understanding eyes, and thereby transformed into sense and wisdom while, however, losing none of the enchantment and love of freedom that have led me to write them down.

It is a terribly long time since all this happened, but now, when I have related it anew to myself, I have a decided feeling that it could all happen again, if even in some quite new manner.

I'm laying down my memoir-pen convinced that the wonderful era of Adventure still hasn't passed away after all. (That would be rather sad, don't you think!)

I would like every plucky Moomin to consider my experiences, my courage, my good sense, my virtues (and possibly my follies)—even if he would not care to draw instruction from the experience, which he will one day have to acquire for himself in the wondrous and toilsome way that is characteristic of all youthful and talented Moomins.

This is
THE END
of the Memoirs.

But here follows an important
EPILOGUE.
Turn over!

EPILOGUE

Moominpappa laid his memoir-pen on the verandah table and looked in silence at his family.

"Congratulations!" said Moominmamma with great emotion.

"Congratulations, Pappa!" Moomintroll said. "I think you're famous now!"

"What?" exclaimed Moominpappa and jumped in his chair.

"When people read this book they're going to believe that you are famous," Moomintroll said positively.

The author wiggled his ears and grinned.

"Perhaps!" he said.

"But then, what happened then?" cried Sniff.

"Oh—then," replied Moominpappa and made a vague sweeping gesture that took in the house, the family, the garden, Moominvalley, and generally everything that follows after one's youth.

"Dear children," said Moominmamma shyly, "then everything *started.*"

A sudden gust of wind rattled the windows. The rain increased.

"To be out at sea on a night like this," mumbled Moominpappa abstractedly.

"But what about *my* father?" Snufkin asked. "The Joxter? What became of him? And of Mother?"

"Yes, and the Muddler!" cried Sniff. "Did you lose the only father I ever had? Not to speak of his button collection and the Fuzzy!"

There was a silence on the verandah.

And at that exact moment, singularly enough, at the very moment needed for this story—there was a rap on the door. Three hard, short knocks.

Moominpappa jumped to his feet and cried, "Who's there?"

A deep voice answered, "Open the door! The night is wet and cold!"

Moominpappa threw the door wide.

"Hodgkins!" he shouted.

Yes, in onto the verandah walked Hodgkins. He shook the rain off himself and said, "It took some time to find you. Hello."

"You're not a day older!" cried Moominpappa

ecstatically. "Oh, what happiness! Oh, how glad I am!"

Then a small, hollow voice was heard to say, "On a night of fate like this the forgotten bones rattle more than ever!" And the ghost itself climbed out of Hodgkins's knapsack with a friendly grin.

"Happy to meet you!" said Moominmamma. "Would you like a glass of rum punch?"

"Thanks, thanks," Hodgkins said. "One for me. And one for the ghost. And a few for the others outside!"

"Have you brought somebody?" asked Moominpappa.

"Yes, a few parents," Hodgkins said with a laugh. "They're a little shy."

Sniff and Snufkin went rushing out in the rain, and there stood their fathers and mothers, getting cold feet because of

the weather and because they hadn't sent word for ever so long. There was the Muddler holding the Fuzzy's paw, and each of them had a button collection in a large valise. And there was the Joxter with his pipe gone out, and the Mymble crying from emotion, and the Mymble's daughter, and thirty-four small Mymbles, and especially Little My (who hadn't grown at all), and when they were all inside, the verandah was filled to bursting point.

It was an indescribable night.

Never before has any verandah held so many questions, exclamations, embraces, explanations, and rum punches at the same time, and when Sniff's father and mother at last began sorting out their button collections and gave him half of them on the spot, everything became so agitated that the Mymble started collecting her children and hiding them in the cupboards.

"Silence!" cried Hodgkins and raised his glass. "Tomorrow . . ."

"Tomorrow!" repeated Moominpappa with youthfully shining eyes.

"Tomorrow the Adventure will continue!" cried Hodgkins. "We'll fly off in the *Oshun Oxtra*! Everyone! Mothers, fathers, and children!"

"Not tomorrow, tonight!" cried Moomintroll.

And in the foggy dawn they all tumbled out into the garden. The eastern sky was clearing, waiting for the sun to rise. It was at the ready, in a few minutes the night would be over, and everything could start anew from the beginning.

A new door to the Unbelievable, to the Possible. A new day when everything may happen if you have no objection to it.